CW00704160

The Forgiveness Quilt

An Amish Christmas Carol

J. Willis Sanders

This is a work of fiction. Names, characters, organizations, places, events, and incidents are either products of the author's imagination or are used fictitiously. Any resemblance to actual persons, living or dead, or actual events is purely coincidental.

No part of this book may be reproduced, or stored in a retrieval system, or transmitted in any form or by any means, electronic, mechanical, photocopying, recording, or otherwise, without express written permission from the author, except for brief quotations in a book review.

Copyright © 2022 J. Willis Sanders

All rights reserved.

ISBN: 978-1-954763-46-3 (paperback)
ISBN: 978-1-954763-47-0 (ebook)

BUGGS ISLAND BOOKS

Printed in the United States of America
Cover art by bookcoverzone.com

By J. Willis Sanders

The Eliza Gray Series
The Colors of Eliza Gray
The Colors of Denver Andrews
The Colors of Tess Gray

The Forgiveness Quilt: An Amish Christmas Carol

Coming in 2023:
The Clara Engelman Series
Clara's Mourning
Clara's Courtship
Clara's Choice

The Outer Banks of North Carolina Series
The Diary of Carlo Cipriani
If the Sunrise Forgets Tomorrow
Love, Jake

The Hope Series
The Coincidence of Hope
The Yearning of Hope
The Gift of Hope

Writing as J. D. James
Reid Stone: Hard as Stone
Reid Stone: Red Rage

Readers: please enjoy the first chapter of *Clara's Mourning* at the end of this book The entire Clara Engelman Series will be published in 2023. The first chapter of *The Essence of Emmaline Strong* is also included. This novel is now available.

Verified Amazon reviews for The Colors of Eliza Gray

"Captivating! ... J. Willis Sanders has captured love in this story. Love of a father to his daughter, love between brothers and sisters, and true love struggling to find a way to a future together. I look forward to Sanders' next book."

"I can honestly say that "The Colors of Eliza Gray" had me hooked from chapter one! It had me wishing for a "happily ever after" for Eliza from the beginning. Every emotion is found in this book and J. Willis Sanders definitely knows how to draw his readers in! I had read half of it before I realized it and finished it up the next morning!"

"Enjoyed this book so much! Stayed up way past my bedtime to finish it. Romantic and inspiring story. Great descriptions enabling the reader to visualize the scenes. Highly recommended."

"You won't be able to put this awesome book down! Love, love of a father and their love!!!! Please write another about how their lives are going!!!"

"The Colors of Eliza Gray is one of the most compelling books I've ever read. Beginning with a hearing-impaired abused Eliza. Taking you through her education and life altering experiences once she has her world opened to her. I truly hated it to end. Can't wait for the next book."

Foreword

Many readers know the Charles Dickens story, *A Christmas Carol*. With its iconic Ebenezer Scrooge and Tiny Tim, it has touched many a heart since its publication in 1843. Within its pages, through visits by the spirits of Christmas Past, Present, and Future, Scrooge must face his own faults and learn how important kindness is.

In my story, we meet Ruth Raber, an elderly Amish woman who must face her own faults. Of course, as difficult as it may be, facing our faults is the ideal. Whether we are Christian or not, religious or not, we cannot better ourselves if we refuse to recognize our faults and grow from them.

Dickens knew this and wrote about it. Not only did he write about facing our faults, he wrote about England's treatment of the poor, including how a person who owed money was sometimes placed in debtor's prison, like his own father was, where the person had no chance of earning a way out.

Dickens also wrote about the plight of orphans, reflected in their treatment in England at the time. He also used his writing to critique how, at that time, wealth affected status and, therefore, class. In my opinion, and possibly in Dickens' opinion too, neither wealth nor the lack of wealth creates class; only kindness creates class.

At about 30,000 words, Dickens wrote *A Christmas Carol* in six weeks. I set out to do the same and managed about 27,000 words of a first draft in about six weeks. I am happy with the results. Ruth is every person, and I hope we can all learn from her. So now I offer you this story of Christmas, of kindness, and most of all, of forgiveness.

(And thanks to my daughter for helping with the final edit so I could get this published before Christmas. It's MUCH appreciated.)

J. Willis Sanders

11/30/2022

The Forgiveness Quilt

Chapter 1

Like a glowing ember pulsing with heat, the dull pain in Ruth Raber's lower back flared and dimmed, flared and dimmed. She rolled over in bed to face the window, where the *tic-tic* of sleet and a gray dawn announced a new day. Taking her equally gray braid in her fingers, she started to loosen it but stopped. After cleaning the house so thoroughly yesterday, she deserved a few more minutes beneath the warm covers. Besides, the brightening light outside meant the sleet was mixed with snow, which must have blanketed the yard overnight. This meant she had no intention of harnessing Lucy to the buggy and going anywhere for anything.

Her left hand, seemingly on its own, slid to the other pillow to find the head of the husband she had never married. For the time it took to blink an eye, despair entered her heart, until gratitude for *Gott's* love forced it away. Just opening one's eyes every day was a blessing. One could hurt, cry, hunger for love and companionship here on earth, or one could find the positive in all things. Ruth knew this was difficult for her to do, but she didn't quite know why.

Breath rasped in her throat. Her chest rose and fell, rose and fell. Birthdays and more birthdays. How old was she now?

At sixteen, at her first gathering, when the youth of her community attended singings to find a potential husband or wife to court, she had sat across from the table from Thomas Yoder. He wasn't particularly handsome, but her parents said he was a hard worker who had already decided to forgo *Rumschpringe* and be baptized into the church as soon as he turned eighteen. This was acceptable to Ruth, therefore her decision to sit across from him.

Then, without a word, he had moved to another table.

Ruth did the same thing for every singing until her eighteenth birthday, choosing a different boy each time with the same results each time. That summer, as she walked home behind *Daed, Mamm,* and Timothy, her *bruder,* she prayed and prayed to understand the boys' lack of interest in her. She read the Bible often. She went to church with her family each and every time. She had learned to cook and clean and sew and make baskets and garden as well as any other girl in her community, but none of that made any difference.

Wind howled around the corners of the house. Branches from the oak outside her bedroom clattered against the wall. In their stalls in the barn, Lucy whinnied and the milk cow mooed. Their water was frozen and they had eaten their hay and feed. The weather was even keeping the rooster in the henhouse. Big Red himself didn't care for winter any more than Ruth did, evidenced by his lack of crowing.

In the window, the light grew brighter. The snow must be several inches thick by now. The *tic-tic* of the sleet stopped. A beam of sunlight burst through the glass, illuminating the curtain: thin, white, and plain. Then the sky faded back to gray. Huge snowflakes, like drifting leaves coated with frost, followed, visible even through the thin curtain. Other than *Gott,* who knew how deep the snow would get before it ended.

The horse whinnied and the cow mooed again. Better get up and tend to them before the snow deepened.

As Ruth rolled over to sit on the side of the bed, the pain in her back stabbed deep into the muscle, making her gasp. Her breath rasped again. Her heart galloped wildly in her chest. *I'm ready when you call, Lord. Other than existing on this earth, I've had little reason to come into this world.*

Another pain, this one in her chest, said a heart attack might happen at any time. The thudding boom in her ears said a stroke might occur as well. The dark growth on her nose said skin cancer might take her also. Only the Lord knew which one it would be.

Wearing the black leather shoes and black dress and bonnet of her Old Order Amish community, she donned a heavy coat and opened the back door. A gust of icy wind swirled snow beneath the porch. Despite the edges of the bonnet extending past her face as if she were peering from within a dark tunnel, flakes stuck in her eyebrows, melted on her cheeks. She almost slipped and fell on the steps but kept her balance. The snow came to her ankles, an icy crust of sleet crunching on top. One step, two steps, five. She shook her head. Her gloves, she had forgotten her gloves. Her arthritic fingers would be numb in minutes without them.

Ruth …

She looked up into the multitude of snowflakes, each as large as a hen's egg. She started to ask who had called her name, but a gust of wind stole the words from her freezing lips. The cancer must be growing in her brain; either that or old age was making her senile. Yes, indeed, what use did she have on this earth any longer? No beloved husband warmed her heart, her home, or her bed. No beloved children, grandchildren, or great-grandchildren visited on Thanksgiving or Christmas to say how much they loved her, to say how fine a cook she was, to say, "What would we do without you, *Mammi?*"

Her shoes left trenches in the snow. Twice, she almost lost her footing in the crust of sleet. Behind her, the wind clattered the oak limbs as if they were the bones of

Daed and *Mamm,* long dead now.

At the barn, when the deepening snow wouldn't let her open the door enough to allow any light inside, she shook her head again. She had forgotten a kerosene lamp.

Ruth …

Through the narrow gap between the barn door and the wall, she peeked into the darkness inside. No one here. No one outside. Her grasp on reality must certainly be slipping.

The horse whinnied. The cow mooed. Regardless, she must have a lantern to find the pitchfork and —

Ruth shook her head again. The wooden cover over the well would be heavy with the snow and sleet, and the horse and cow needed water.

Ruth …

Breathing hard, each breath a cloud pluming from her mouth and nostrils, she squeezed through the narrow opening and stepped inside. Dust assailed her sense of smell, hay and manure too. To her left, somewhere in a corner, a mouse—or worse, a rat—scurried in the darkness. Despite the dim light penetrating the cracks in the overlapping boards here and there, each illuminating a haze of dust motes, Ruth couldn't see the pitchfork. Running her hands along the walls, she felt everything but: a shovel and a hoe for gardening, a rake for gathering oak leaves in the fall, a scythe for cutting corn stalks after the golden ears were picked.

She stopped to lean her aching back against the horse's stall door. Lucy whinnied and snorted; the cow mooed.

Ruth had no idea why she hadn't named the cow. Maybe she should now, before she died and the cow's new owner didn't know what to call her. A hoarse laugh erupted from Ruth's throat. What a silly thing to think. If she died out her in the barn, she wouldn't be able to tell anyone the cow's name.

She shivered. Her hands were freezing, fingers stiff. Even inside the barn, with what little light was available, she could see her breath cloud before her face. Inside the leather shoes, her toes were numb.

A gust of wind moaned. The barn's tin roof rattled. The oak limbs clattered. The door slammed shut, blown by the wind. Except for the light entering those cracks in the walls, darkness surrounded her. Fear clenched her throat. Terror gripped her heart. She gave a little cry—the cry of a child in the night afraid of the dark, hot tears streaming, soaking her pillow.

Whose memory was that? Certainly not hers. Or was it? Yes, but not the cry of a child. Rather, it was the cry of a young woman seeking—yet not finding—love. She remembered the afternoon Thomas Yoder moved to another table. At home that night, as she unpinned her hair, she studied her reflection in her bedroom window. Her eyes were honey-brown like the soil in her family's garden—a good thing. Her nose was upturned—cute as a button so *Daed* said—very nice so *Mamm* said. In private, years before, Timothy said she resembled a pig.

Several sings later, that night at home, *Daed* and *Mamm* whispered in their room about Ruth being too plain to attract a boy. At the window, she studied her face again. Timothy was right; she resembled a pig.

In bed, as tears streamed past her ears and wet her hair and pillow, she dreamed of a voice. *Ruth,* it called, *true beauty lies within the heart and soul through faith. Do not believe otherwise. A person who doesn't know this will make the years long and the heart lonely.* Those beautiful, booming words ended her tears. She climbed out of bed and knelt on the hard, wooden floor to thank *Gott* for his insight, and to ask forgiveness for her doubts.

In the stall, Lucy pawed the straw while the cow bumped the wall with her hip. Ruth shuffled to the barn door and shoved it open. She went back to get the shovel and slowly made her way to the well. After breaking the crust of sleet and scraping the snow from the wooden cover, she fetched the bucket from the barn, filled it and took it to the porch. Warm up inside first, then care for the animals. She stomped her feet, leaving little piles of snow gathered around her shoes. In the kitchen, she opened the door to the wood stove and almost cried. She had forgotten to add wood before bed last night, and the fire was nothing more than a few glowing embers the size of a fingernail. Even worse, she hadn't brought any wood inside or to the porch. Of course, it was stacked beneath a tarp behind the barn, another treacherous trip away.

Ruth, they're counting on you, you know. Don't let them down.

Ruth jerked her head up and glared at the ceiling. "If that's you, Lord, I'm sorry for my infirmity. I'm doing the best I can. Isn't that all anyone can do?"

No answer. No booming voice. Nothing but the near silent crackle of those few cooling embers sending a wisp of woodsmoke curling upward inside the stove.

Wary of her sore back, Ruth dragged a chair over from the kitchen table and eased into it. Snowmelt glistened on her shoes. She held her hands over those barely pulsing embers. Once her hands were warm, she might be able to water and feed the animals, gather wood and make breakfast, including a pot of steaming coffee. With plenty of sugar and cream, it was her one weakness.

She frowned sourly, feeling the wrinkles in her face fold. No, her other weakness was always believing she resembled a pig, like Timothy had said.

Her hands gradually grew warm, the fingers becoming flexible. Sleep tugged her eyelids down. Sleep or death, whichever it was, she would welcome it.

Ruth, the booming voice said, *let's visit a Christmas past.*

Chapter 2

What felt like a summer breeze rippled through Ruth's clothing. She shrank in the chair until her feet, now bare, weren't touching the floor. Her hands were much smaller: smooth instead of wrinkled, clear instead of dotted with age spots, knuckles normal instead of swollen with arthritis. Her heart thumped confidently, not hesitating, in perfect rhythm.

Youth, she thought. *I'm dreaming I'm young again.*

She glanced around the room. She was still in her kitchen, except it was the kitchen of her childhood. Sitting at the huge table, the oak planks hewn by *Daed, Mamm* was stitching swatches of cloth together to make one of her Wedding Ring quilts. Making several each year, she gave them as Christmas presents to newlyweds, the elderly, and to people amongst the *Englisch*.

Ruth once heard the bishop tell *Mamm* the quilts were too extravagant a gift, that the appreciation of the recipients of her skill could lead to her having prideful thoughts. *Mamm* clucked her tongue and told the bishop that if having appreciation for *Gott's* gift to her of being able to make quilts was pride, so be it. The bishop's mouth fell open. His cheeks above his long, gray beard turned pink. Laying a finger aside of his nose, he thought for a moment and then told *Mamm* she had made a fine point.

This happened at an after-singing meal one day when Ruth was seventeen. Like all the singings, no boy sat across from her, and Thomas Yoder was sitting across from Susan Stoltzfus. Everyone expected him to walk her home eventually, but he hadn't yet. Ruth hoped he never would. Why did Susan deserve happiness over her? Besides, Timothy said Susan resembled a pig too, especially when she smiled. Thomas didn't seem to think so; he always returned her smiles. He even ate more than one slice of her shoo-fly pie even though it looked like something the milk cow plopped to the ground in the pasture. Ruth considered adding some of that to the pie for real to see if Thomas liked it but never did. Instead, she practiced her own cooking in hopes of Thomas, or some other boy, trying it one day.

That Christmas, Thomas told his parents he and Susan wanted to court. Every time Ruth was alone, she cried and cried. She had always held hope in her heart for happiness with him, but her hopes had failed her.

No, her hopes hadn't failed her, she thought at times. *Gott had failed her by giving her a nose that made her resemble a pig.*

Ruth, the booming voice said, *how old are*

you in this Christmas past?

Ruth looked around the room. *Mamm* still sewed. In one of the rocking chairs by the fireplace, where a small wreath made of running cedar hung on the mantle, *Daed* read the Bible by the flickering lamp on a table by his side. Timothy, in the other rocker with a wooden horse that *Dawdi* Raber had carved, stuck his tongue out at her, then pushed his nose upward to make it look like pig's nose. Seeing all this, Ruth realized she was seven years old and Timothy was eight. If she recalled correctly, he had first made the comment about her nose last summer.

So, Ruth, the voice boomed, *tell me what you did that night to your bruder for his teasing.*

Ruth said nothing. She hadn't done anything to Timothy. Breaking his toy horse had crossed her mind. So did putting horse manure under the quilt at the foot of his bed. Instead, she'd silently fumed, her forehead hot enough to sizzle bacon.

Still stubborn I see, the voice said, this time not so booming.

Again, Ruth said nothing.

Timothy clambered from the rocking chair and padded in sock feet to *Daed.* "Will you read the Christmas story to me?"

"Luke, you mean. Climb up in my lap." He faced Ruth, eyes gleaming in the lamplight, his beard dark against his white shirt. "I have room for you too, Ruth."

On the floor with one of her faceless dolls, Ruth shook her head. *Daed* flipped pages in the Bible. His deep voice seemed to vibrate in the air. *Mamm* glanced over and smiled. She didn't smile at Ruth.

The moment hung in time: the faceless doll, *Mamm* sewing, *Daed* reading, Timothy snuggled in his lap, yawning now and then.

Ruth poked at the doll's face where the nose should be. Before she went to bed that night, she took a pair of *Mamm's* scissors and cut a hole where the doll's nose should be. Now she would never resemble a pig, and a boy would sit across from the table from her at a singing one day.

As *Daed* continued to read to Timothy, *Mamm* called Ruth over. She gave her a needle and asked her to thread it because her eyes were tired. On her knees on the wooden bench, Ruth propped her elbows on the table and leaned near the kerosene lamp. Its oily fumes made her wrinkle her nose. Done with the needle, she studied *Mamm's* fine stitching on the quilt. It looked like hard work: squinting and poking the needle in and out, over and over again through the squares of cloth with batting between them until a quilt large enough for a huge bed was completed.

Like all the rest, this one was made with interlocking rings, which confused Ruth. "*Mamm*, why do you make Wedding Ring quilts when the Amish don't wear wedding rings?"

Mamm straightened in the ladderback chair. "To me, circles mean the continuation of love in a marriage, and the love *Gott* means for marriage to be, like the love Jesus has for us all. Forgiveness is a circle too. When we repent—I mean *truly* repent, not just say we repent—*Gott* forgives us. Even then, though, we sometimes can't seem to forgive ourselves. When that happens, it separates us from His plan for us in life."

Ruth paused to take in this information, but she still didn't understand. To her, the rings on a quilt were just for looks. To her, her life, since Timothy had said she resembled a pig, and since later, *Mamm* and *Dad* had said she was too plain to attract a boy, was a straight line destined for loneliness. She had always thought this, from this day so long ago to now, as an elderly woman. She stood from the table. "*Gott*, if you're the voice I've been hearing, I'd like to go home now. I'm used to being alone. People just hurt each other. Their words don't mean anything. Only the Bible is the true word."

Mamm, rubbed a small circle between Ruth's shoulder blades. "You seem troubled, sweetheart. Can I help?"

A single tear formed in the corner of one of Ruth's eyes. Still in the chair with Timothy in his lap, *Daed* looked at her. "Come join your *bruder*, Ruth."

Timothy slid over in *Daed's* lap. "We've got room. *Daed's* getting to the best part."

Ruth blinked. The tear ran down her cheek. She looked away, toward the ceiling and around the room. "I want to go home, *Gott*. Of all the cows and horses I've had over the years, none have ever said they would accept me when they didn't mean it. All they needed was a pat on the head to start their day. Then they knew I would feed and water them, and we all were happy."

The air shimmered. A winter wind kissed her cheeks. She was sitting by the wood stove again, her hands clasped just outside the open door. The weight of age sank into her joints and muscles. The pain returned to her back. Her knuckles were swollen and stiff again. She touched her cheek where the tear had left a wet trail only a moment ago, but it was dry. *Just a dream,* she thought, *more like a nightmare.*

The cow mooed. The horse whinnied. Ruth slowly rose from the chair. She needed to get wood for the stove and make coffee to get her going. Once her insides were warm, her outside could perform the rest of her chores.

In the yard, the snow filled the air like feathers from a pillow fight she and Timothy once had. *Daed* didn't even get angry about it. When he caught them, he fell on the bed and laughed, happy to see both *bruder* and *schweschder* happy.

This time her shoes left deeper trenches in the snow. The wind howled harder. More snow stuck in her eyebrows and melted on her cheeks. The oak limbs clattered louder, still reminding her of the bones of *Daed* and *Mamm.*

At the wood pile, it took too long to scrape the deepening snow off with the shovel. Inside Ruth's chest, her heart burned from exertion. Inside her sinuses, it felt like someone had forced ice water up her nose. In her throat, someone had taken an ice pick and driven it through her neck and into her spine. She sank to her knees until she caught her breath and rose again.

She did this over and over until enough wood for today and tonight was stacked on the porch. At the stove again, as she sat to warm her hands, freezing because she had forgotten her gloves again, she did cry at the sight of the embers, now nothing but cooling ash.

The horse whinnied; the cow bellowed.

Ruth gathered kindling and struck matches. A small fire soon crackled. When the flames reached higher, she added three sticks of the icy wood but left the door open to sit and hold her hands outside it again.

For the most part, satisfaction filled her

youth. Happiness, another thing altogether, eluded her. Children avoided her. When this started, she couldn't recall. Try as she might, she couldn't pull the memories from her muddled mind. They were there, though, hiding like children in a summer game of hide and seek, of which she had never partaken. Why the neighbor children shunned her, she didn't know either, but they did. She would wait at the edge of the yard, sweating in her black dress and bonnet. Squealing boys and girls ran back and forth to cries of "I see you! No, you don't! You better run faster before I catch you!" Ruth just waited and sweated, eyes burning with tears. They didn't want her, the girl who resembled a pig. They never asked her to play and she never offered. Why do so when they would just say no?

Hands warm, Ruth closed the stove door. She filled the coffee pot with water from the pail on the counter, added coffee and set it on the stove. In the chair again, she watched the glass bubble on top for the telltale sign of boiling water transforming into delicious coffee.

A whisp of steam, white and ethereal, like the ghosts of her past, soon rose from the spout.

The unmistakable sound of a diesel engine rumbled in the driveway. Through the window over the basin, Ruth saw the man who brought wood, driving his pickup truck stacked high with split oak. She always bought enough to last a year, so why was he bothering her now? Waiting at the screened door, she crossed her arms as he came up the steps and knocked snow off his boots. "Morning, Ms. Raber. With this storm and all, I thought I'd see if you needed more wood."

"Don't I always buy enough to last the winter?" Ruth asked, forgetting his name.

The man removed his baseball cap, not a proper hat like the Amish wear. "Like I said, I thought …" He sniffed. "Is that coffee I smell? I've been delivering wood all morning and sure could use a cup."

Ruth was appalled. No Amish person would expect to be invited into a home like this, virtually barging in.

The sheen of moisture shined beneath the man's nose, which he wiped. He sniffed again, licking his lips, no doubt, at the aroma of Ruth's coffee. "Well, if you don't need any wood, I better get going."

Although he said this, he didn't put his cap back on. Typical *Englischer:* no manners, no kindness, just the expectation of others doing as they say.

He pressed the cap over his graying hair. "It'll be Christmas in a few days. If you don't mind me mentioning it, I never see you going anywhere for it or anyone coming here."

Ruth said nothing. Where she went, or who came here, or who *didn't* come here was none of his business.

He blinked and worked his lips in and

out. "Well, I suppose I'll see you next fall for your usual load of wood. Merry Christmas."

Although Ruth slammed the heavy wooden door shut as the man drove way, the rumble of the diesel engine assaulted her senses. No, she couldn't smell the bitter exhaust from the *Englischer's* truck, but she could imagine it, having smelled it before.

She poured coffee, added sugar and milk and sipped while scrambling eggs. Bacon, ham, or sausage would be wonderful, but she preferred living frugally over splurging. Biscuits, however, baked in the oven section of the wood stove, would've been wonderful, with the rich yellow of eggs over easy, if she had remembered to cook them that way.

Done with her meal, Ruth shook her head. Not only did she need to force herself out into the blizzard to feed and water the horse and cow, she had to feed the chickens in the henhouse and gather their eggs.

Within the haze of her memories, one grew clearer. *Ruth,* the booming voice said, *let's visit another Christmas from your past.*

Chapter 3

Still sitting at the table with her plate, Ruth looked around. Perhaps the cancer on her nose—if it really was cancer—had burrowed into her brain deeper than she had thought. Regardless, her chores were more important than an imaginary voice demanding she make melancholy visits into her equally melancholy childhood. She waited, though, wondering if she would be whisked away like the last time the voice boomed. When she wasn't whisked away, she guessed it really *was* the cancer burrowing into her brain, or perhaps, like anyone who didn't know *Gott*, she could either choose to believe in the booming voice or not.

Not a woman to leave chores undone, she washed her breakfast dishes and the pan in which she had cooked the eggs. As far as the coffee cup, she rinsed it only, expecting to have more coffee later, the pot keeping warm on the edge of the wood stove.

In the henhouse, as snowmelt on her bonnet soaked her hair and wet her ears, she slipped four eggs from beneath the warm bottoms of six hens and eased them into her apron pocket to avoid breakage. Big Red strutted around. His red comb tilted this way and that as he eyed the empty water and feed pans. "I know, Red, I know," Ruth told him. "I'm a bit slow this morning. I'll get to it soon."

Unceremoniously, as well as unexpectedly, Red strode to her, paused at her feet, peered into her eyes, and focusing on her shin, aimed a sharp peck at it.

Ruth squawked. The hens squawked. Red took aim again, and Ruth kicked him across the henhouse. "Peck me, you old buzzard, will you? I'll wring your neck and fry you for supper if you ever do that again."

A hot rush of blood heated Ruth's face. Her *Ordnung* said to never, under any circumstances, resort to violence. She eyed the two peck marks on her shin, both dotted with blood. But did that include when an ornery rooster was trying to peck her to death?

A second rush of blood heated her face. Red hadn't been trying to peck her to death. Like Lucy whinnying and the cow bellowing, Red was hungry and thirsty, and his actions were Ruth's fault for not tending to him or the hens. He never did that before, though, and Ruth had been late rising at other times. *Well,* she thought, *I should forgive the old rascal anyway, and I can start by getting him and the hens their food and water.*

Outside, she gathered snow and left it in the pan to melt. In the barn, she scooped feed into one of *Mamm's* cracked bowls and took it to the henhouse to empty into the pan.

You can't ignore me forever, the voice boomed. *Think back and tell me if you recall an event in your life concerning chickens. You know the one.*

In the henhouse, like in the barn, streaks of light pierced several spaces in the boards, carrying galaxies of dust motes that floated about. The hens pecked feed, evidenced by the metallic clank of their beaks striking the pan. Big Red scooped water in his beak and raised his head to let it run down his throat.

The scene brought back a kernel of memory. Ruth hadn't thought about it in forever, having closed it off like closing a door on her chances of a finding a young man with whom she could share her life.

Down the road about a mile or so, where an Amish couple and their large family lived on a huge farm, their middle daughter obsessed over their chickens. This in itself wasn't odd. Many Amish children, Ruth included, enjoyed petting the hens and naming them, but Naomi spent hours each day with them.

Her parents didn't mind. In fact, they urged her to do so. The result was the finest hens in the community and a daughter who was happy despite her upper lip being split. *Daed* said it was called a cleft palate. *Mamm* said the only word Naomi ever attempted was her name, which sounded like Yomie.

Other than the strange appearance the split lip gave her, and her lack of speech, Naomi did the same things other Amish girls did. Even at sixteen, she joined her first sing to search for a boy to court. Ruth never expected her to find anyone. Not only did she have a cleft palate and couldn't speak, her plain features—dull, brown eyes, dull, brown hair, a narrow nose like a chicken's beak, and an equally narrow face—made her resemble an actual chicken. When she was a child during hide and seek, neighbor children flapped their arms and squawked at her. She never reacted, though. She just kept running around and smiling as if she didn't have a care in the world.

What galled Ruth more than anything was how, at Naomi's very first gathering of the youth, Lloyd Miller, inarguably the handsomest boy in the community, with brilliant blue eyes and a smile to match, and blonde curls to his ears, sat right across from Naomi and smiled at her. Of course, like any Amish girl with any sense would do, she smiled back. He walked her home that afternoon, and two years later, on the first Tuesday in November, they were married.

For the life of her, Ruth didn't understand it. She'd overheard enough boys to know they preferred pretty girls, or at least those who didn't resemble a chicken and couldn't talk.

Lloyd worked hard and saved his money. Before Naomi turned twenty-five, he asked her if she would like to have surgery to fix her lip. By this time she was speaking more, although the only people who understood her were those close to her. She said if *Gott* wanted her to be born without a lip like hers, she would've been, to please use the money to add a room onto the house for their next child, who he didn't know about. He flung his wide-brimmed straw hat into the air and picked her up and swung her around, kissing her at the same time.

As a neighbor told Ruth the story, she tried to imagine it but couldn't, tried to understand it but couldn't, tried to speak to *Mamm* about it later but couldn't.

For whatever indiscernible reason, *Gott* had chosen to bless Naomi far more than he had chosen to bless the girl who resembled a pig.

The sudden strike of Big Red's beak in the feed pan startled Ruth back to the present. Like with her memory of *Mamm* sewing a quilt and *Daed* reading the Christmas story in the Bible to Timothy, why was she thinking about the past so much?

Since the best way to forget the past was to think about the present, Ruth left the henhouse for the barn.

The snow still fell, coming halfway up her shins. The wind howled worse than before, clattering the oak limbs terribly. Even the tin on the barn's roof banged as if it might rise up and fly away. On the way to the barn, slogging through the thickening snow as if it were molasses, Ruth grabbed at her black bonnet as a gust of wind snatched it from her head and carried it away. Three steps later, the pins came loose from her bun. In three more steps, the wind blew her hair around her face and shoulders: a curtain of iron-gray cobwebs.

Again she told *Gott* she was ready to die. Life held no spark for her anymore, not that it ever had.

Inside the barn once more, Ruth found the bucket for the cow and horse's water and made her way to the well.

The temperature was dropping,

evidenced by her breath transforming to a white haze as soon as she exhaled. Upon arriving at the well, she dropped the bucket. The well top was covered again, and she'd left the shovel at the woodpile. Instead of venturing back, she clawed the snow away with her fingernails. When she was done, her hands and fingers were blood-red and numb from the cold. She tried picking the bucket up by the wire handle, but it slipped from her grasp over and over again.

The horse whinnied, this time adding a snort. The cow mooed, this time adding several mournful bellows. Ruth sat in the snow and leaned against the wooden wellhouse. She raised her hands and blew to warm them, but the wind sucked her breath away from her mouth before it reached her hands. Cupping them over her mouth, she blew again and again. Although her hands warmed somewhat, her lungs felt as if someone had shoveled a fire's glowing embers inside them.

She raised her eyes to the sky, to the blizzard, to the swirling snow and asked *Gott* to take her now. No one would miss her because no one cared like they had never cared. She would freeze and remain here until the storm ended and the sun came out. When she thawed with the next warm spell, crows and vultures would pick her bones clean. In the spring, when she was fully exposed, the coyotes would carry her bones into the woods, cracking them to extract the marrow for their pups.

Ruth didn't mind these things. She would become part of *Gott's* plan for nature. In a way, although the crows and vultures and coyotes weren't people, they would cherish her and the part she played in their lives. At least that was a certain kind of caring, even if in death.

She had played no part in anyone's life. In her mid-twenties, when it was painfully obvious no young man would ever care for her, she had stopped attending church.

Mamm, Daed, and Timothy, married then, begged her to come. Timothy's wife, Anna, begged her to come. Their son, Timothy Jr., said, "Please come, Aunt Ruth. Everyone asks about you all the time."

Ruth's reply never changed. "I read my Bible on the Sabbath and pray. I don't need people to do that. *Gott* is with me. He is my friend."

Over the years, two different bishops, three different deacons, and all their wives had visited Ruth singly and together. They made small talk, apparently afraid to openly broach the subject of her not coming to church by saying, "Ruth, you need to come to church to worship with us." Instead, after the small talk, they spoke in parables: "We're a community and *Gott* is our shepherd. If a sheep ventures out on its own, the wolves will kill it. Like the men building a barn, we're stronger together than apart. Like the women cooking the after-church meal, we nourish each other better as a family instead of as one."

Ruth rarely responded. When she did, she patted the Bible in her lap and said, "The Lord and His word is all I need. You can be on your way now."

Snow gathered on Ruth's dress. It turned from black to gray to white. Flakes swirled, some brushing her eyelashes. The world was awash in windblown white. Despite her predicament, she continued blowing on her hands until she could feel the bucket's cold, wire handle.

Snow fell from her dress and head as she stood. Her arthritic knees popped. Her back throbbed. She filled the bucket halfway—any more would be too heavy to carry—and shuffled through the deepening snow to the barn, where she entered the door still ajar. Thank *Gott* she had left it that way, or she would've never gotten in.

She fed and watered the cow, returned to the well and fed and watered the horse. In the house again, she sat by the hot stove with another cup of coffee. Perking up after a sip, she chuckled. "It seems my old body is still strong, Lord. Maybe I've got a few more years left in me yet."

You think you're ignoring me, don't you, Ruth? You're not, you know. I've gotten through to much harder heads than yours.

Ruth chuckled again. "Whoever you are, you better bring a hammer. This old noggin is too tough to crack."

In a hurry for the coffee, Ruth hadn't taken off her bonnet and coat, now dripping on the floor. She shoved a chair close to the wood stove and draped the coat across it to dry. She did the same with the bonnet. She then retrieved a dishtowel and sat again to squeeze the water from her hair. It took three towels until she could pin her hair up and cover it with another black bonnet from her bedroom. Done with that chore, she traded her soaked shoes and socks for dry ones. The thick coat, one of *Daed's*, had kept her dress dry, thank goodness.

She added another stick of split oak to the stove, warmed her coffee and sat again, this time with a fried apple pie leftover from supper last night.

Mamm made the best fried apple pies. Every fall, when the Winesaps and Golden Delicious and Granny Smiths filled the orchard on the other side of town, the red, yellow, and green globes hanging from heavily laden limbs, *Daed* would hitch the horse to the wagon and everyone would pile in for the ride. On the way, as the horse's shoes *clip-clopped* along the road, Ruth and Timothy would start by standing behind their parents. By the time they got to town, they would sit in the back with their feet hanging off. As they passed the grocery and the post office and the hardware store, Timothy waved, grinning as if the *Englischers* strolling the sidewalks and crossing the street were friends. Regardless of his joy, Ruth, her face enveloped by the black bonnet as if she were looking from the dark confines of a groundhog hole, refused to wave. Dressed like a flock of bluebirds mixed with yellow butterflies mixed with red cardinals, *Englischers* must be the proudest people alive. With their heads cocked back, they waved at Timothy as if to say: *That's right, I'm important and I know it. That's why I wear these colorful clothes, so I can catch your eye.* Even *Mamm* and *Daed* waved, confusing Ruth. After all, hadn't she heard them calling the *Englischers* fancy folk?

And then there were their vehicles: cars and trucks in all shapes and sizes, most with shiny paint that reflected the autumn sun, from apple red to summer-sky blue to snowflake white and all shades in between, the drivers with their heads thrown back in the same haughty angle as the *Englischers* striding the sidewalks and crossing the streets, wearing pride in their fancy vehicles in their gleaming eyes: *Look at me in my car or truck you don't have. Aren't I something and aren't you nothing in your silly horse-drawn wagon, living in the past instead of in the future?*

During these rides through town, Ruth never failed to wrinkle her nose at the bitter smell of vehicle exhaust. When people waited for the wagon to pass, she sometimes smelled perfume and deodorant and cologne, having sniffed each in a department store once, when *Mamm* went for thread for her quilts. Once had been enough. Not only did the *Englishers* demand adoration with their clothes and vehicles, they even demanded it with how they smelled.

These actions puzzled Ruth to no end. Didn't they know those worldly things carried no weight with *Gott?* He valued faith above all, both in Him and in His precious Son.

These memories continued to draw her into her past. Before she knew it, she was sitting beside her *bruder* again, hanging her feet off the wagon, watching the *Englishers* pass, smelling the smells, scoffing at their fancy clothes and shiny vehicles, and looking forward to arriving at the orchard, which an Amish family from another community owned

The jostle of the wagon stopped. The *clip-clop* of the horse's shoes faded. An invisible hand, its fingers hard and bony like the skeletal limbs of the clattering oak outside her bedroom window, grasped Ruth's throat and squeezed. Another grabbed an ankle and pulled her from the wagon, landing her in the middle of the road outside of town. She leapt to her feet and ran into a corn field; the dried stalks and leaves clattered like the skeletal limbs of the oak. The sky turned dark. Thunderheads bloomed overhead like black roses, an impossibility on *Gott's* earth. Behind her, those skeletal fingertips struck the dried cornstalks, no doubt spreading them while searching for Ruth.

She ran until her lungs burned, until her

heart drummed, until she tripped on a stone and fell face down in the weeds and grass between the rows of dead cornstalks.

The rattle of skeletal fingertips striking the cornstalks came closer. *Well, my little Amish girl,* a voice hissed, *here you are, trying to hide from the sins of your past. Rise and face them, lest I drag you down into my home of fire and brimstone to meet my master.*

"No!" Ruth cried, pressing her face into the weeds and dirt. "I'm not a sinner, I'm not a sinner, I'm not a sinner. I love *Gott* with all my heart. Please go away. Please leave me be. Please take one of those wicked *Englischers* instead. They deserve to be taken to your master."

The voice laughed, a sound like the screech of woman gone mad. "Deserve, you say?" he now said, his voice echoing around her. "Don't all humans deserve those flaming pits, sinners that they are?"

"Not if we repent!" Ruth screamed. "Not if we repent!"

An unearthly chuckle answered, one which gripped Ruth's guts with a spasm of nausea. "Now we get to it, little Amish girl. When shall you repent?"

Ruth didn't answer; she had nothing to repent for. "Please go away. I love *Gott* and His Son. Please ... please go away."

"Go away? I can no more go away than I can repent for you, child. You'll carry your sins until the day you die, it seems, which may not be far from now. Now rise and remember, for only then can you avoid those flaming pits."

The clattering of the corn stalks ended. The weeds pressing into Ruth's face became grass: lush, thick, and smelling sweetly as if it had just been mown. A buzzing sound turned her head. A voice opened her eyes. *No,* she thought, *I can't bear this scene from my past. Take it away, Lord. Please take it away.*

A hand took hers and pulled her up. The hand was warm yet calloused. "Wake up, sleepyhead. I didn't invite you to a picnic to have you ignore me by pretending to sleep."

Pulled to a sitting position, her legs tucked beneath her, Ruth opened her eyes. She and the boy were sitting on a Wedding Ring quilt in the middle of the orchard in springtime. Joy replaced dread. Happiness replaced heartache. Innocence replaced guilt.

Blue sky stretched from horizon to horizon. Bees buzzed and dipped into apple tree blooms. Bluebirds warbled and sang while flying from limb to limb. A spring breeze, deliciously warm and soft, caressed her face.

The boy raised his palm to her cheek, and Ruth closed her eyes.

The middle son of the orchard owner, his name was Ethan Peachy. They had met the previous fall, when *Mamm* and *Daed* came for apples. In the strict definition, he wasn't handsome, but his smile illuminated his face like a summer sunrise over the rolling Ohio hills.

He removed his wide-brimmed straw hat and placed it on her bonnetless head. With his hand still on her cheek, he pulled her to him. This was to be their first kiss. He had talked her into removing the bonnet, saying he wanted to see her honey-brown eyes and smile. She had offered both, a gift she had never considered giving before marriage.

Regardless, the thought of a kiss before marriage drew her away from him and made her throw his hat to the quilt. "I'm not that kind of girl," she said. "And I didn't know you were that kind of boy."

Sitting back, he chuckled. "You brought this quilt for our picnic. I only wanted to thank you." He ran his fingers through his auburn hair, green eyes grinning. "This is our third date, and I haven't seen a genuine smile out of you yet. Why is that?"

Ruth bared her teeth. "There."

"Not bad. You never welcome me either. No, 'hello, Ethan.' No, 'good morning, Ethan.' No, 'how are you, Ethan?' No, 'thank you, Ethan, for providing our lunch.'"

Ruth pointed at two pieces of pound cake wrapped in wax paper. "I brought dessert."

The bees buzzed. The bluebirds warbled. The warm breeze blew.

"Yes, you brought dessert, but it takes more than pound cake to make a relationship. Do you understand what I'm saying?"

"I hitched the horse to the buggy and came all the way here." Ruth didn't say the rest: *and I lied to Mamm and Daed for each date, saying I needed thread to make my own Wedding Ring quilt.*

Ethan shook his head. "I suppose you don't understand."

"I know what the Bible says about marriage."

"I know that too," Ethan said impatiently. "I also know what it says about simply being kind to each other. 'Ephesians 4:32 - And be ye kind one to another, tenderhearted, forgiving one another, even as *Gott* for Christ's sake hath forgiven you.'"

Ruth folded her hands in her lap. "Bringing cake was kind."

Ethan crossed his arms. His nostrils flared. His eyes narrowed. He gathered all the food in the basket he had brought and stood, red-faced. "No, you don't understand." He started to turn away to leave but turned back. "You might not believe me, but I really wanted to get to know you. When I saw you, I thought, 'who is this shy girl hiding in her black bonnet? Why does she never raise her head? Why does she never smile? What happened in her life to make her forget to be kind and tenderhearted?'" He took several steps and turned again. "Have a nice life, Ruth. Somehow I doubt that will happen."

"I don't need you!" Ruth yelled. "All I need is *Gott* to have a nice life."

Ethen tilted his head to one side. "Those tears in your eyes say you don't understand what *Gott* needs from *you*. I'll walk you to your buggy if you'd like."

Ruth shook her head. "*Gott* needs my faith. What else is there?"

"Like I said, you don't understand."

Ruth lowered her head to palm the tears from her eyes, pressing so hard she felt the bones beneath her cheeks.

The bees no longer buzzed. The bluebirds no longer warbled. The warm breeze no longer caressed her face. The swish of the grass from Ethan's bare feet announced his departure.

Unable to comprehend what he had said she didn't understand, she folded the quilt and took both it and the cake to the buggy.

At home, *Mamm* asked why she hadn't bought the thread. *Daed* asked why she had taken two pieces of cake and a quilt. Without a word, Ruth left both on the kitchen table and went to her room to kneel by the bed. Footsteps crept to the door she should've closed. "What's wrong?"

Timothy asked. She should've faced away so he couldn't see her face. "Are you crying?" he asked.

Ruth wanted to tell him pigs didn't cry. Instead, she pressed her face into the bed and silently wept.

His footsteps padded closer. A hand rubbed a gentle circle between her shuddering shoulder blades. He was fifteen now, a strapping boy with a deep voice. "Come now, *schweschder*, it can't be that bad."

She told him to go away, told him to not tell *Mamm* or *Daed*. He asked what was wrong, asked if he could help, asked if anyone had harmed her.

Only you, she wanted to scream.

Minutes passed. The gentle hand left her back. His footsteps left her side. The door hinges squeaked as it closed.

Neither *Mamm* nor *Daed* came to see about her, more evidence that they didn't care for her the same as Timothy—or none at all.

Instead of praying, Ruth climbed beneath the covers and buried her face into the pillow to muffle her sobs.

Something warm and wet soaked Ruth's lap. She emerged from her daydream to see she had spilled the coffee from the cup she was holding in her hands.

How long had it been since she had thought of Ethan Peachy and the orchard and that terrible day?

She used a towel to wipe the coffee from her dress and refilled the cup.

Not long enough.

Chapter 4

The rest of the day passed agonizingly slow, as if Ruth were waiting for someone to die. Done with the coffee, she left the chair for another stick of oak for the stove. On the porch, she stared at what should be enough wood for the night, but only a few sticks of the split oak remained. Hadn't she stacked plenty of wood there this morning? The only tracks in the snow were those covered trenches she had left while going to the henhouse, to the barn, to the well, and to the back of the barn, where she kept the year's supply of wood under the tarp, so no *Englischer* had stolen the wood on the porch. Also, the tracks of the man who brought her wood, plus his vehicle tracks, were completely covered by the still deepening snow.

A sudden gust of wind, howling like some dying creature in the night, rattled the barn's tin roof. A trip to the wood pile was needed, but a body might get blown over and covered with snow in no time at all. Maybe she had forgotten to get enough wood. After all, she was either losing her grip on reality or the cancer on her nose was burrowing into her brain.

Inside again, with the remaining sticks of wood popping and crackling in the stove, Ruth decided on an early supper. Despite her advanced age, she enjoyed a good appetite, possibly a sign of an impending number of years to live in such an insufferable existence.

Two pork chops soon fried in a cast-iron pan, blackened with time and use. Fresh coffee steamed in the pot, the glass bubble on top revealing the gurgling brew. Biscuits rose in the wood stove's oven, the aroma of browning bread wafting about the room. Green beans bubbled in a pot, a chunk of ham hock seasoning them. Ruth's mouth watered with expectation. Another leftover fried apple pie, warmed in the oven after taking out the biscuits, would hit the proverbial spot, especially with more coffee. Frowning, Ruth shook her head. With the memory of the day at the orchard still ringing in her mind, perhaps she would forgo a fried apple pie.

She sat at the table to fill her plate: a pork chop with a crispy crust, nice and brown; steaming green beans, a piece of the ham hock on the side. Licking her lips in anticipation, she reached for a biscuit without looking, and only managed a handful of air.

Across from her. *Daed* offered a plate of biscuits. "Here you go, Ruth. Butter one while it's hot."

Next to *Daed, Mamm* offered the butter.

To Ruth's right, Timothy offered honey. "Here you go, Ruth. I know you like honey on a hot buttered biscuit."

"That's very kind of you," *Daed* said to Timothy. "You're setting a good example for your *schweschder.*"

Ruth shoved the jar of honey aside. "I don't care for any today."

"Ruth," *Mamm* said, her voice stern. "Your *Daed* and I taught you to be polite. We thank each other in this house when someone is kind."

Ruth lowered her head. From within the black bonnet extending past her face, she stared out of its dark tunnel. When had anyone in this house ever been kind to her? To *Mamm* and *Daed,* she was plain. To Timothy, she was a pig.

"Take that bonnet off," *Daed* ordered. "You're not outside and it's not cold. Your *kapp* will do."

Forks and spoons clattered to plates. Glasses raised and lowered, thumping softly to the table.

"Do as your *daed* says," *Mamm* said. "We can't see your face."

"I'm not hungry. May I be excused?"

"Only if you're going to your room to pray for forgiveness," *Daed* said, his voice as stern as *Mamm's*

Ruth blinked. Back in the present, she stared at her fingers. They hung in the air above one of the biscuits she had baked for her early supper.

Forcing the memory of yet another awful day aside, she buttered the biscuit. She had not eaten a drop of honey since *Mamm* and *Daed* had shamed her, and she never would.

The pork chop was tough. The green beans were salty. The biscuit lay like a lump of cold dough in her stomach. The coffee did nothing to warm it. She put away the leftovers, washed and dried the dishes, and returned to the chair by the stove to open her Bible.

On the small table to her right, the orange

flame in the kerosene lamp flickered, possibly from a draft from the blizzard still howling outside. Instead of rising to the ceiling, the bitter fumes burned her nose.

Ashes to ashes … dust to dust.

Ruth shivered. *Not that memory again,* she begged. *I cannot bear it.*

The eerie sound of singing reverberated around her. Shovels scooped from the mound of Ohio soil, the smell rich in Ruth's nostrils. Clods of it thudded to the wooden coffin.

Ashes to ashes … dust to dust.

Ruth shivered once more. *Please, no, I cannot bear it.*

A hand took her by the elbow and led her away from the grave. "Heaven has gained another angel, Ruth."

As they walked through the cemetery, threading their way through the gravestones etched with gray, green, and brown webs of lichen, fog clung to the frostbitten grass. For an October day, the weather was unseasonably warm. A misting rain fell, blending it and the fog into one.

As always, even now at forty-two years old, Ruth kept her head down. The mist beaded on her shoes and the grass brushed it off, leaving wet streaks on the black leather. Timothy walked beside her, Anna and their two children at his side. "I wish we didn't have to attend the meal," he said. "I'd rather go home and mourn by the wood stove."

Ruth felt the same way. They passed a maple tree, its remaining leaves bright scarlet. Several drifted down past her face. The limbs at the crown of the tree, bare and extending into the sky with its bony reach, gave the impression of a huge, multi-fingered claw. She could feel it around her neck, could feel it squeezing her throat, could feel it pulling the very soul from her body.

Ashes to ashes ... dust to dust.

And be ye kind one to another, tenderhearted, forgiving one another, even as Gott for Christ's sake hath forgiven you.

"It's just so sad," Anna said.

"I'll miss *Dawdi*," their daughter, Sarah, said, three years younger than Timothy Jr., now fifteen.

Mamm, who had been speaking with the bishop, caught up to them. "Everyone has been so kind." She raised an envelope. "Our community gave us a generous offering."

"Why?" Ruth asked. "You said *Daed* left enough money to take care of us for a long time to come."

"It's our way, the way of kindness. Families make a community, and we help one another in our times of need."

"But we don't *need* it."

"Imagine that," Timothy mumbled, "not even able to feel gratitude for a gift. How can you be so unkind?"

Nearing the buggies, Ruth detoured toward the road. "Where are you going?"

Mamm called after her.

Ruth said nothing. Shouldn't they be able to understand the pig was going home to root in its trough?

Her stride in the driveway lengthened. The gravel beneath her shoes crunched. Footsteps crunched behind her own, and someone draped a quilt around her shoulders. "Use this for your walk, sweetheart. It'll keep you warm and dry in this mist and fog. We'll stay dry in the enclosed buggy when we come home."

Stopping, Ruth gazed up from inside the black tunnel of her bonnet at *Mamm*. She was so kind and understanding, a wonderful *mamm*. Why had her daughter turned out so differently?

Mamm gave her a quick hug. "I know we're all brokenhearted. It was your *daed's* time, like it'll be our time one day. We just need to be ready when *Gott* calls."

On the walk home, as *Englisch* vehicles roared by, leaving windblown mist buffeting Ruth's body and face, she couldn't understand why she hadn't cried during this entire ordeal. Although *Daed's* heart attack had been sudden, he lingered in bed for week, denying further medical care. "If *Gott* has chosen this as my time, it's my time. Our way—the Amish way—is acceptance, and I must accept this."

When *Mamm* didn't get enough sleep from waiting on him, Ruth did so dutifully. By the flickering light of the lamp on his nightstand, she read to him from the Bible. By the light of the midday sun, she lifted his head with one hand while holding a spoonful of vegetable soup to his lips with the other. By the light of the midnight moon, full and yellow, she gave him sips of water, chilled with ice from the icebox. Each time she tipped the glass, condensation dripped to his beard, long with streaks of gray, until she placed a towel there to catch the droplets.

Once in a while he would chuckle. "Now

you get to take care of me like your *mamm* and I took care of you when you were a baby. How we loved you and love you still, Ruth. We have a world of hopes for you, and we pray together each night for you to find your way."

Ruth lowered his head to the pillow and sat in the bedside chair: an old ladderback *Daed* himself had made. "I never lost my way, *Daed*. I read the Bible and pray and work hard and—"

He removed his fingertips from her lips, where he had pressed to end her words. "As odd as it may seem to hear me say it, there's more to life than those things." He patted the Wedding Ring quilt covering him, one of the first *Mamm* had made. "For we are the children of *Gott*, with lives to live as He would have us live, with kindness never-ending, a circle from beginning to end, returned to us in kind—kindness to kindness to kindness everlasting."

Ruth puzzled over his words. "I never

heard that Bible verse. Whose is it?"

Daed chuckled softly. "Why, it's mine. Do you understand what it means?"

She folded her hands in her lap. "Well, it's about being kind."

"And?"

She shrugged. "Is there more?"

He patted her knee. "Think on it and let me know in the morning. I'm ready to get some sleep." He closed his eyes and tried to press his trembling hands together to pray, but as soon as the palms touched, they fell to the quilt. Ruth stood and pressed them together for him. He smiled at her and closed his eyes again. "Dear Father, though I may soon leave my family, please be with them always. Especially be with my darling Ruth. Show her thy way, oh Lord, for it is as clear as the meaning of the rings on all the many quilts my dear wife has made over the years. Amen."

Ruth crossed his hands on his chest. They were still there in the morning, when she found him dead.

Mamm's end had been similar, except it was from a third stroke, twenty-one years later at the age of eighty-three.

Like with *Daed,* Timothy and his family had visited and helped as often as they could. Anna didn't even mind emptying the bedpan or bathing *Mamm's* pitiful body, shriveled and thin, the bones protruding from beneath parchment paper skin, veins crossing the tops of her hands like blue spider webs.

The first stroke five years earlier had weakened her left side. Regardless, she managed to gather eggs and feed the hens and Big Red, the twelfth rooster in a long line of Big Reds. The remaining chores fell to Ruth, for *Mamm's* priority after feeding the chickens and having breakfast was making more quilts.

Two years later, in the middle of night, not uttering a single word, she suffered the second stroke. In the morning, Ruth found her dressed but with her hair down. She didn't have the heart to mention it, although she thought she should: hair coverings were too important to ignore. Regardless, when she saw the right side of *Mamm's* mouth drooping and the listless look in her left eye, she let it go. As *Mamm* shuffled toward the egg basket on the table, Ruth took her arm and steered her toward one of the rocking chairs by the wood stove. "You sit, *Mamm*. I'll do the chores this morning."

"I shpose ah should," *Mamm* said, slurring her words. She pointed to the kitchen table, which meant she wanted to work on her quilts. Ruth didn't see the harm. She settled her in a chair, brought her sewing kit and her latest quilt, made her a cup of coffee, and left for the chores, saying she'd make breakfast when she was done.

Although Ruth hadn't attended church in years, *Mamm* had rose when the services were scheduled, cooked for the meal after, and had Ruth harness the horse to the buggy for the ride. She never failed to ask Ruth to come. Now she couldn't climb into the buggy, so every Sunday, to Ruth's dismay, meant she wouldn't have time to herself.

In spring, summer, and fall, she would take long walks on the farm. Sometimes she strolled the fields where *Daed* once raised sheep. Sometimes she entered the oak, maple, and hickories, where *Daed* and Timothy had hunted deer and turkey each fall. On rare occasions, after placing the mail in the pocket of her dress, she continued down the road, if for no other reason than to get a glimpse of the outside world.

In the spring, the fields offered many treasures: nests of baby rabbits, found when their *mamm* bounced away if Ruth got too close; wildflowers such as wild geraniums, their five wide petals a delicate shade of soft purple; Virginia bluebells, their upside-down blooms powder blue, each resembling an umbrella open in reverse;

and Ruth's favorite, the ever-present buttercup, their tiny petals glowing yellow in the sunshine.

Summer seemed to dim those treasures, both in the fields and in the forest, but within the fields, where thorny blackberry vines offered their first fruits in July, bobwhite quail called: *bob-bob-white, bob-bob-white, bob-bob-white,* and at dusk, as the shadows lengthened and the horizon dimmed and the night sighed with the first breath of cool air, whippoorwills echoed their mournful cries: *whippoorwill, whippoorwill, whippoorwill,* each ending with a rising tone on *will,* as if saying, hey, *you*—hey, *you*—hey, *you.*

In the forest in summer, ticks crept and mosquitoes whined in the emerald-green depths, so Ruth waited until fall, when the days cooled and the foliage hinted with yellows, oranges, reds, and every shade between to announce the season. She loved the simplicity of kicking the crunchy leaves aside, their aroma similar to tobacco curing in a barn, and if she spied the white tail of a deer as it leapt between the trees, or the arched back of a squirrel on a limb, or the pink feet of a mourning dove grasping a branch, so much the better.

She also waited until fall to stroll the road that fronted their farm, preferring this time to study the gardens of neighboring farms. Then again, it wasn't so much the gardens as the families harvesting in their gardens. Seeing *mamms, daeds,* and children held a certain curiosity for her. After all, the only family she would ever have was her own, and they were dwindling in number.

In the time following *Mamm's* first and second stroke, needing to get out of the house to take a break from the constant care, Ruth continued her walks, including on the road. *Mamm* never failed to wave her away when she mentioned these walks, and Ruth was glad. Being cooped up in the house with an invalid was like a dying hen being cooped up in the henhouse: no sun visible, no soft breeze felt upon the skin, no aromas of nature entering her nostrils. On occasion, a soldier returning from what Timothy called the Korean War passed her on the road. Some were missing an arm or a hand. Some wore jagged scars upon their faces. Some either limped or dragged a foot. Some missed a leg altogether and used crutches. Their eyes stared ahead or down, never darting toward her. Ruth couldn't imagine war, but she could imagine how these men might feel, as empty as she felt when she considered her life, wasted away without a husband and children to love.

On one such walk, when Ruth was about a mile from home, no neighbor houses visible, one of these soldiers stopped her instead of passing. He bore no injuries and smiled broadly. "Why, hello, ma'am," he said. "How are you this fine day?" Ruth stepped to one said to pass him, and he blocked her way. "Aw, now, don't act that way," he said, leaning over to peer inside the tunnel of her bonnet. "I'm just on my way home from the war, and I haven't seen a face as pretty as yours in over a year. What's your name? Mine's Albert. How about we walk to town and have a bite at the diner? I'd love to listen to a lady talk a while."

Ruth blinked once, twice, and once again. Of all the words he had said, the only ones she had heard were him saying she was pretty. She raised her chin. "I'm Ruth. What did you say your name is?"

"Albert, ma'am, it's Albert. My folks live on the other side of town. I hitchhiked here from the train station. The train was early, so they're not expecting me until nightfall. I'm just dying to sit at the diner with a pretty gal like yourself and hear your Dutch accent. How about it?"

Studying the man, Ruth wondered how old he was. Crow's feet deeply etched the corners of his eyes, and a few gray hairs were scattered in his brown hair at the temples. He wasn't a young man, but neither was he an elderly man. As she continued to wonder, the man again smiled broadly.

"I'm sure you're wondering how a man my age—sixty if you'd care to know—served in the war, plus how he doesn't have a wife and children and grandchildren to go home to. I never married is why. My folks are in their early eighties, and I'm an only child. I was a career Army man, a captain in the war. Does all that help?"

The part about being a captain escaped Ruth. "What does a captain do? I see you're not hurt."

"Oh. You mean like other men you've seen walking to town."

"That's right."

Lowering his head, Albert rubbed his chin. After a moment or two, he raised it. "Sorry to say, us captains give orders." Like the wind moaning in the leafless oaks on a winter night, his voice carried a note of melancholy. Ruth guessed he might've ordered men to their deaths, the reason for his sadness at her question.

He clapped his hands and grinned, revealing even, white teeth. "Enough of that. Won't you come to town with me and have a bite at the diner?"

Ruth considered the question. Members of her community might see her with this man in town, and she didn't want that. She lowered her head again. Why was she considering his request—her, an Amish woman who had taken the vows to her community's church? They weren't supposed to socialize with outsiders, also called fancy folk, were they? And hadn't *Mamm, Daed,* and Timothy often chastised her for not being kind? And hadn't they also spoken with the *Englisch* in town? And hadn't *Mamm also* given many a quilt to many of those same fancy folk for Christmas? Since this was the case, why not be kind to this older gentleman? He obviously carried the weight of sending men to their deaths on his shoulders, so why not share a meal with him if it eased his burden? She shared her concern about being seen in town, and he nodded with understanding. Then she asked if he would like lunch in the barn, and he heartily agreed, beaming his bright smile again.

On the way to her driveway, he whistled while he walked, and Ruth could feel the unbidden hint of a smile on her lips. This was what it felt like to walk with a man who thought she was pretty instead of thinking she resembled a pig—and an *Englischer* at that.

When they passed Ruth's closest neighbor, an Amish man in her community, he stopped harvesting turnip greens and stood to touch the wide brim of his straw hat. "A fine day, is it not, Ruth?"

"Very nice," she said, hurrying along.

"Who is this man with you?"

"He's lost. I'm walking him as far as my house. Then he can continue to town on his own." Like an icy winter wind, both lies sent a thrill through Ruth's blood. They had come so easy—*too* easy. What did that mean for her, an Amish woman committed to *Gott* and all He stood for?

"Well, it's kind of you to help this *Englischer*," the neighbor added. "I hope you both have an enjoyable time."

Still hurrying along, the black dress flapping between her ankles, Ruth looked back at the neighbor. Chuckling and shaking his head as he knelt to continue harvesting turnip greens, he winked at her. If she didn't know any better, he was having unclean thoughts about her helping Albert. How dare he!

"You know," Albert said, "I understand how the Amish don't make a habit of socializing with town people. If you'd rather I go on to town by myself, I can."

Although a still, small voice warned her

about her lies, Albert's tender voice ended any concern. "It's all right. I would enjoy talking to you. My *Mamm* is sick, and I don't see many people."

"What about your dad?"

"He passed away long ago."

"And your brothers and sisters?"

"A brother. He married and moved to his own farm."

"If you're sure ..."

"I'm sure."

In the barn, Ruth settled Albert on a rickety chair at *Daed's* workbench and said she would be back soon with their meal. *Mamm* was sitting by the wood stove with a cup of coffee, the rocker tilting back and forth. On the table, the half-finished quilt waited. Ruth went to her. "Are you going to take your afternoon nap?"

Mamm raised her partially closed eyes to her. With her usual slurred speech, she asked if Ruth enjoyed her walk. "Very nice," Ruth said, trying to keep impatience from entering her voice. *Mamm* then asked if Ruth knew she had made ten quilts in the years after her first stroke, adding how she truly had gratitude to *Gott* for giving her those skills, adding also how she wished she could share the quilts she had made as Christmas gifts like she did before the strokes.

"I'm going to have my lunch in the barn," Ruth said before Mamm said something else. "We have leftovers from supper last night. Can I warm anything up for you?" *Mamm* glanced out the window and said if Ruth helped her out to the porch, they could eat there in the fresh air.

Ruth heated four biscuits, placed slices of roast chicken on them, and filled one small and one large glass with lemonade from the icebox. She placed one biscuit and the small glass on the table beside *Mamm*. "It's getting chilly out, you eat in here." *Mamm* answered with downturned eyes but did as she was told.

In the barn, Ruth offered Albert a biscuit and took one for herself. "We'll have to share a glass. The rest are dirty."

About to take a bite of the biscuit, he lowered it. "All the glasses are dirty? I thought Amish folks kept their homes tidy all the time."

"We … people came over for supper last night," Ruth lied, amazed it had popped out so easily.

"Oh. Well, shouldn't we say grace? I'm sure the Amish do that before every meal."

Ruth took a bite of biscuit, chewed, swallowed, and drank lemonade. "I'm hungry, aren't you hungry? I thought you were hungry."

Albert lowered his head. "Dear Lord, thank you for this meal and thank you for Ruth. Despite my many sins in the war, I know you understand I was doing my duty. I tried hiding them in the back of my mind, but that still, small voice kept telling me to repent and be forgiven, and I have. In Jesus name we pray, amen."

After another bite of biscuit, Ruth stopped eating. "Um … do you really think I'm pretty? I'm sixty myself, far from being a girl like you called me."

Drinking lemonade, Albert lowered the glass. "I didn't ask, but aren't you married? I thought the Amish valued families?"

Ruth didn't care to explain this. No man had ever told her she was pretty, and she wanted to know why he thought she was. "We value families. I just didn't find the right man."

Albert took another bite of biscuit, chewed and swallowed. "This is delicious. It's been a while since I had home-cooked food." He followed with lemonade. "Do you mind taking your bonnet off? It's like talking to someone inside a tunnel."

Ruth did so, revealing her white prayer *kapp*, and set the bonnet on the workbench.

"There now," Albert said. He chuckled. "Now I feel like I'm talking to a lady instead of a groundhog looking out of its hole. You really are quite attractive. You could pass for forty-five any day of the week, maybe even forty. Why, if the Amish were allowed to date us town folks, I'd take you out to dinner and a movie, or dinner and dancing, not that our little town has a dance hall."

From hearing *Englischers* in the town grocery, Ruth knew about movies and dancing. If not for her community's *Ordnung*, she wouldn't mind seeing a movie. Dancing, though, she could do without. In 1945, when World War II ended, people in town played their car radios and stomped in the street as if their feet were on fire and they were trying to put them out. They whooped and hollered too, exactly like she might if her feet were on fire. She understood it to a degree: the end of any war was something to celebrate. She had parked the buggy back a way and watched, curious about the wiggling and hollering, the beat of the music and the way it welled up a rhythm inside her, like when the twin streams of milk from the cow sang against the inside of the metal pail.

Then a different song played, slow and smooth, the singer's voice silky and sultry. Before Ruth knew it, she was swaying back and forth on the wagon seat, eyes closed, feeling as if the man singing was caressing her face with his words.

"My, my." Albert chuckled. "What in the world are you thinking about, Ruth? You're flushing like a teenager."

Ruth pressed her palms to her cheeks, which were quite warm. "Oh, nothing. Nothing really."

Grinning, Albert said nothing. When their food was gone, he stood and took her by the hand. "Would it be wrong to ask you to dance, oh, Amish maiden?"

Ruth pulled her hand away. "I shouldn't."

He took her hand again. "Why not? We only live once, so why not experience something you'll never experience again?"

Ruth's cheeks flushed even warmer. Here she was, an Amish woman of sixty, never married, never kissed, never loved. What was so wrong with one dance from this, by all accounts, decent man?

She stepped close to Albert. His eyes smiled. The crow's feet crinkled. "I'll hum us a slow tune," he said. "I don't care for all that wiggling around like the young folks do these days." He slipped his right hand around Ruth's waist, raised her right hand about shoulder high with his left hand, and hummed a tune similar to the slow tune on the radio Ruth had heard.

Her head came to his nose. She could feel his warm breath on her forehead. Before she realized it, she had lain her head on his shoulder and was holding him tight. *So this is what it feels like to be loved?* she thought. *What an amazing thing, yet what a sad thing to have never experienced this feeling in all of my life.*

Albert stopped humming and led her back to the other chair by *Daed's* work bench. Like on butchering day, when the men gathered to process hogs for meat and lard, Ruth felt as empty as one of those carcasses, as if someone had yanked her insides out. Part of her wanted to beg Albert to hum again, to hold her again, to—as ashamed as she felt to think it—take her to the hay loft and lie down with her as married couples do. If he did, she might have an idea of another one of those things in life she had missed.

Albert sat in the other chair. "You know, I accepted Christ as a boy, but over the years I often wondered if my faith was real. When I got older, around fourteen or so, I'd comb my hair certain ways and wear certain clothes like the popular boys in school did. In general, I made a fool of myself because I was worried about what other people thought of me." He rubbed his chin. "About a year ago, when bullets were flying around my head, I got to praying about all that. Then I realized how some boy teasing me about my acne ruined my confidence. All in all, I think it ruined my faith too, if I ever had it to start with." He tapped his chest with a fingertip. "When I got through praying, my heart felt like it was going to burst with happiness. I was still sad, though. I had let some teasing boy bother me, even to the point of ruining my faith and not finding a special lady to love because I was so shy."

Ruth wondered why he was telling her all this. It had nothing to do with her. She stood. "Can we dance again, Albert. I loved it so much."

He glanced at his watch. "It's been a fine time, Ruth, but I need to hit the road to see my folks." At the barn door, he turned. "Thanks for lunch and the dance. Maybe I'll see you around town sometime."

He turned to leave, hands in his pockets. When he passed the mailbox and took a left toward town, he started whistling an upbeat tune. His stride widened, and soon he was a tall, slender figure half a mile away.

Another chapter in Ruth's life had offered a glimpse into what might've been, and now that chapter had ended. Stinging tears tempted—sobs too—but what was the use? Not only was she alone, she was too old to start life over. After *Mamm* died, she might as well die too.

Several shuffling steps later, Ruth crossed the yard, climbed the porch steps, and entered the house, the screen door squeaking open and squeaking closed behind her. At the table, bent over the quilt, a thread and needle in hand, *Mamm* turned to ask if she had enjoyed lunch in the barn. Saying nothing, Ruth took the dish and glass to the basin to wash.

Despite having faith as a child and honoring it from then on, she had wasted her life. Since that was the case, why had

Gott forsaken her? Hadn't she deserved love, marriage, children, grandchildren, even great-grandchildren, all gathered around her at Christmas, possibly to take turns sitting in her lap as she read the story of Jesus's birth in Luke?

Apparently she didn't deserve a thing, having left any chance of loving her own husband and children behind years ago for whatever reason.

All around Ruth, the air shimmered like moonlit fog on a summer night. With her next breath, she found herself back in her rocking chair, the Bible in her lap, the aged and spotted hands of an eighty-year-old woman clutching the worn leather binding.

A chill gripped her, either from the oak in the wood stove burning to embers or from her soul shriveling into a hint of its once youthful self, when hope of love, now gone forever, had filled her heart.

Chapter 5

The next morning, after Ruth woke to press her warm feet onto the icy floor, she dressed while peering out the window at the crescent moon, glaring down from a black sky. At least the snow had stopped, but the moon seemed to taunt her with an evil grin: *That's right, old woman. You forgot to bring more wood to the porch before bed. Now the house is as cold as a grave.*

Shivering at both the thought and the freezing house, she dressed and went to the kitchen to don her coat hanging on a peg by the door, then gasped as she stepped outside to the porch.

Not only was the house as cold as a grave,

the air outside was too. Every breath seared her sinuses with cold beyond cold. It was even too cold to form a cloud of white before her face, for as soon as she exhaled, it dissipated as if it were spirit, either ascending upward to Heaven or descending below to—

Part of Ruth didn't care to think about the place below, where demons wait for the unrepentant sinner, but part of her did. She started to question that part, but as the first syllables of the first words formed on her trembling lips, she spat onto the oak boards of the porch, vowing to never think that question again.

Th dry snow crunched beneath her shoes. The layer of crystalline gray reflected the partial light of the grinning moon. She raised the kerosene lamp, which sent a pool of yellow light ahead of her. Before she reached the woodpile behind the barn, her black dress wore a hem of powdery white, as if someone had dipped her in sugar.

At the stack of split oak, she placed a gloved hand there to rest. The cold air burned her throat and lungs. Her heart clattered in her chest as if it were a dying engine in one of the *Englischer's* tractors. Whether here, by the well, or in the yard, one of those places might welcome her body soon, becoming a grave to eventually be discovered by the man who would bring the wood next fall. More snow would cover her. She would become an indistinguishable mound until spring. Someone driving along the road might notice a bit of black clothing fluttering in the wind, or they might not. No one cared about the crazy old Amish woman who lived alone and never married, who never came to town unless she ran out of coffee, sugar, flour, or anything else she might need. Who would care about anyone who resembled a pig? Not anyone she knew.

Regaining her breath, Ruth made three trips to the porch with three sticks of split oak, each bundle cradled in her left arm and pressed to her chest as if it were the baby she would never give birth to, the baby she would never love.

Why so much regret now? It piled upon her soul. With each step her knees throbbed; her back ached; her arm cradling the wood cramped.

At the porch steps with the last load—last because she could hardly breathe—her knees and back gave way, and she collapsed to the steps. The wood clattered across the porch. Two pieces settled; the other rocked back and forth, back and forth. The aroma of sawdust on Ruth's coat reminded her of wood cutting day with *Daed* and Timothy: the scrape of the file on the teeth of the cross-cut saw, their breaths puffing white in the October air, morning frost sparkling in rainbow hues in the yard.

A burst of sunlight from over the eastern horizon illuminated Ruth's immediate world in red, orange, yellow, then white.

For all she knew, hours had passed while she lay on the steps covered in snow.

Behind her in the barn, the horse whinnied, followed by the cow's moo. Ruth couldn't remember the horse's name, but she knew the cow didn't have a name. The rooster, though—she knew his name—strutted from the henhouse door. From beneath the overhang protecting the chicken's small yard within the chicken wire fencing, Big Red looked around at the snow. As his red comb flopped to one side of his feathered head, he crowed as if he were cursing the weather, then hurried back inside.

Ruth managed a weak laugh. "That's right, you old coward. Go on back in there instead of facing the world like I have to do every day."

The laugh become a cough. The cough became a raspy wheeze. The raspy wheeze became a dull pain in her chest, which radiated to her left shoulder. She had felt this pain often enough for the past few months, expecting it to become a lightning bolt that extended down her arm, like *Daed* had described his heart attack.

The sun rose higher. Its warmth reached her face, yet the brightness of the new day failed to cheer her spirits. Yes, she would actually die, likely soon, and the thought frightened her to tears. For some reason she couldn't understand, the promise of Heaven in the Bible didn't set well within her heart. She had read it from cover to cover several times over the years, but sometimes it seemed like the words were nothing but chicken scratch, as meaningless as her life had been. This was blasphemy— of course it was—but she couldn't fight the feeling of having missed the most important part of the scriptures. For all she knew, regardless of her vows to her community's church, regardless of reading each and every verse, she might be bound for the world below, in the fiery pits meant for unrepentant sinners, and she didn't even know why.

Pushing up from the porch, she rose on trembling knees. Inside, she placed the last three sticks of wood in the stove, stirred the embers beneath them with a poker until the oak flamed, and closed the cast iron door with a *clank*.

Standing there, she considered every corner of the house, each a place where memories waited like ghosts to grab hold of her and drag her back into the past.

Maybe breakfast, or at least coffee, would give her a better outlook. If not, she knew who the next ghost would be. Fear drew tears again. It was useless to fight what was coming, like it had around Christmas for the last few years, as the end of her life drew near.

Still, she made coffee. Still, she made eggs. Still, she baked fresh biscuits, despite the cold ones wrapped in foil on the counter. Maybe the present could ward off this particular ghost from her past, for it was the worst one yet.

With the meal sitting heavy in her stomach, she washed dishes and stoked the fire. Then, dredging up a sigh from the depths of her soul, she shuffled to *Mamm* and *Daed's* room to meet the next ghost and get it over with.

The door creaked open. Sunlight pierced the space between the white curtains over the single window, leaving a shaft of brightness that illuminated the oak planks at the foot of the bed. Dust coated the chest of drawers to Ruth's right, the dresser without a mirror beside the window, the Wedding Ring quilt covering the bed, the two nightstands with kerosene lamps, the single rocking chair on the other side of the bed. Although no wind blew today, what might've been a draft stirred the curtains and made the chair shudder. A chill gathered at the nape of Ruth's neck and crawled down her spine: either icy fingertips tapping or bony digits scratching.

She walked around the bed and sat. In her wake, in the shaft of light basking the wood floor in brightness, dust motes swirled and danced.

Ruth lowered her head and closed her eyes. Although she couldn't see *Mamm's* face, she opened her eyes to imagine her head lying on the pillow as she slept in the final days of her life.

Before then, after Ruth helped her to the kitchen, she sewed quilt after quilt at the table. No matter how much her fingers trembled, no matter how much she squinted in the yellow pool of light from the kerosene lamp, no matter how much Ruth asked why she was determined to make so many quilts, she continued doing so. Then one day, to Ruth's dismay, she stopped eating and went to bed. No one could make her eat, not even Timothy, so they let her be.

Ruth reached out to place her hand on *Mamm's* hand, where it rested on the quilt covering her in the bed. Blue veins appeared luminous beneath powder-white skin. Cold yet warm, stiff yet supple, the fingers clasped Ruth's hand. "Ah, Ruth," the voice said, weak as a whisper. "I see I'm still here."

Ruth had to listen hard since the third stroke, the words slow and slurred. "Yes, *Mamm*. You're still here." She took a cup of tea from the nightstand. "Are you thirsty? I added honey like always."

The narrow face, skeletal and gaunt, tensed. "Not now, sweetheart, not now." The throat swallowed, evidenced by the faint appearance of an Adam's Apple in the neck, wasted and thin. "I've been thinking about you and Timothy and your *Daed*. Remember the day your *bruder* offered you honey for your biscuit and you said no?"

"That was years ago, *Mamm*. It's not important now."

"I wish your *daed* and I hadn't spoken so sharply to you, but we didn't understand why you were so unkind to Timothy." *Mamm* swallowed again. "We had heard him tease you about your nose, but you were children then. It's as if you held it against him all your life. Is that why you've been unkind to him ... and to ..."

Mamm always grew tired at this point in Ruth's memories, but Ruth never failed to hear the unsaid accusation: *and to ... everyone?*

The chest beneath the quilt rose with the rhythm of sleep. Ruth dozed too, until *Mamm* touched her hand.

"When I was young, I knew a girl who thought she was too plain to find a husband. I asked her why she thought that. She said she overheard someone say that about her." *Mamm* eyed Ruth as if she expected her to admit something. "Don't you think that's a sad story? People say things without thinking—even people we love. They're just thinking out loud, you know. It doesn't mean anything. Anyway, the girl overcame her doubts about finding a husband."

"How did she do that?" Ruth asked.

Mamm patted Ruth's hand. "By praying to *Gott* to remove her doubts. You see, she had to realize how beauty—true beauty—is a gift from *Gott*. True faith helps us realize this, because He loves us all the same. He created us, Ruth, so He loves us regardless of our appearance. That means we are to love each other the same, and to show that love with kindness to one another." *Mamm* raised her head. "Can I have a little tea now?"

With one hand, Ruth supported *Mamm's* head while holding the cup to her lips with the other. After only two sips, when she usually had several, she said she was done. Ruth eased *Mamm's* head to the pillow and set the cup aside. "Would you like to rest now?"

"I would like to know what you think of my story. I wish I had told it to you long ago, but I just remembered it."

Ruth looked away. *Mamm's* story had nothing to do with her. She loved *Gott,* read the Bible, and prayed almost constantly. She didn't question His love for her.

In the shaft of light piercing the space between the curtains, a single dust mote lit like a spark rising from a burning ember.

For the briefest moment, the booming voice blasted inside her head: *It's not my love you should question, Ruth. It's your—*

Ruth forced the voice away. To believe it would mean— No, to believe such a thing would kill her.

"Ah, sweetheart," *Mamm* whispered. "Do you understand my story now?"

"No, *Mamm,* I don't understand it all," Ruth said, not turning to face her.

"Your *daed* and I had such hopes for you. You were such a sweet child. You rode with me to town every time I gave quilts away. You wished everyone who took one merry Christmas and said God bless you. When we got home, after your *daed* unhitched the horse, you asked him to remember to read the story of Christ's birth from Luke after supper. Then, for no reason we knew of, you changed. You wouldn't say what, so we stopped asking you. We hoped you would grow out of it, but you never did. Won't you tell me why you changed now, Ruth? Can't you tell me before I go to meet your *daed* so I can tell him we didn't fail you?"

Still not facing *Mamm*, Ruth clutched her hand. "You didn't fail me."

The same dust mote brightened again. *Now, Ruth, since you told your mamm the truth, who truly failed you?*

In Ruth's hand, *Mamm's* fingers relaxed. Again, she slept. Again, like with *Daed*, Ruth crossed *Mamm's* hands on the quilt. Again also, like with *Daed*, Ruth found her like this in the morning, dead.

The beam of light dimmed until the entire room darkened. The dust mote brightened into the sun over the cemetery, where Ruth stood beside Timothy and Anna and their children, beside the grave with *Mamm's* coffin in it.

"Ashes to ashes ... dust to dust," the bishop said. The people gathered around, at least three hundred, came closer. Many wore *Englisch* suits and dresses. Everyone sang something Ruth couldn't recall. Done with the song, they offered their condolences to the family and left for the church and the meal to follow.

Timothy thanked the bishop and left with his family. The bishop asked Ruth if he could speak to her for a moment. She didn't see the harm, so she stayed.

Three shovels stuck from the mound of earth to one side of the grave. A spring rain, soft and warm, barely enough to wet the greening grass, misted the air and formed droplets on the bishop's black hat and long, gray beard. He placed the Bible inside his coat and crossed his arms over it. For a long while he looked out over the cemetery—a man weighing his words—then faced Ruth.

"I'm sure this is a difficult time, but I hope you can tell me why you haven't been to church in so long. We're a community, and communities treasure each and every member. It doesn't matter if you aren't married and don't have a family of your own, Ruth. Won't you please consider joining us again? We'd love to have you."

The mist turned to raindrops tapping Ruth's bonnet. Had he actually said they would love to have her? No one had ever loved her, nor had anyone wanted to be around her. *Daed* and *Mamm* had cared in a way, perhaps Timothy too, but too much pain had crossed the bridge of their lives to go back now. From within the black tunnel of her bonnet, she looked up at the bishop. "I have everything I need at home to worship *Gott*."

"But you are not worshipping *Gott* with the fullness of your heart." He placed a gentle hand on her shoulder. "You carry a great burden. We all see it in your eyes. You hide behind this bonnet whenever we see you in town. People speak and you don't hear. You are our family. We want to welcome you back with open arms."

Heat flared in Ruth's cheeks—heat and anger. "Why are those *Englischers* here? They don't belong at an Amish funeral."

The bishop removed his hand from her shoulder. "Much has changed in our community over the years, due in large part to your dear *mamm* and *daed.* Your *bruder* fought it at first—others did too—but we have come to love the *Englisch* like *Gott* said to love our neighbors—as we love ourselves."

"But they drink alcohol and commit other sins too despicable to mention. They think they're better than us with their fancy clothes and automobiles. How can we love them?"

The bishop shared a soft smile. "You say you have everything you need at home to worship *Gott.* I assume you mean your Bible also. Do you not read it?"

"Every day."

"Do you understand it?"

"Always."

"I doubt it—not if you don't understand what I said about loving our neighbors as we love ourselves." The bishop looked over his shoulder at the church. "Won't you come in for something to eat? You didn't when your *daed* died. Please do." Pulling down the wide brim of his hat against the increasing rain, the bishop left for the church.

Ruth listened to the splash of his shoes, to the whinny of the horses, to the growling of her stomach. She had spent the last two days going through *Mamm's* things and had eaten little. Why not go in for a quick bite? Regardless, she didn't have to speak with anyone, much less those *Englischers.*

Inside, when she closed the door with a *thump,* everyone turned to watch her. Most held plates of food. Some held glasses. The pews had been moved aside to make room.

She hung her coat and bonnet on a peg and went to a table filled with main and side dishes. The aromas of roast beef, chicken, and pork, plus green beans, butterbeans, boiled potatoes and several types of casseroles rose from the table.

From behind her, someone touched her shoulder. "I'm glad you came in," Timothy said, offering her a plate and utensils. "*Mamm* and *Daed* would be glad too. You've spent most of your life in that house, sheltered away from the world, and it's time you got out."

A bit stooped with age, Ruth looked up at him. "I have everything I need at home."

"Won't you be lonely now, with *Mamm* gone?"

"*Gott* keeps me company."

"You're my *schweschder*, Ruth. I worry about you."

Saying nothing, she filled her plate. He hadn't worried about her when he told her she resembled a pig, so why worry now? She poured lemonade. In an empty corner, she faced a wall and ate, placing the glass on a window sill between sips.

Timothy joined her. "I think the entire town turned out for *Mamm.* She was a special lady, giving away all those quilts." He paused. "She and *Daed* were wonderful parents, always teaching us lessons about kindness, don't you think?"

Ruth said nothing.

He kissed her cheek. "I love you, *schweschder.*"

Ruth watched him join Anna and their children, now grown and with children of their own. As cruel as he had been to her, why had *Gott* blessed him with a family? She faced the window again to continue eating.

"Hello," a familiar voice said. "I'm very sorry about your loss, Ruth."

Ruth spun around, almost spilling her plate, and faced Albert. "You … I didn't see you in the cemetery."

"I was in the crowd. When I heard about your mother, I wanted to see you. I lost my folks a while back, so I know how it is to be alone." Albert paused, his eyes appraising her. "How have you been?"

Ruth placed the glass on the window sill. "I'm making do, I suppose."

"I'll always remember our little dance in your barn, and the lunch you fed me. It was a nice welcome home."

The bishop came over. "Hello, Albert. Do you know Ruth?"

Albert shared a soft smile with Ruth. "Oh, we're just fellow travelers on the road of life. I found my way shortly before I left the Army, but I think Ruth got sidetracked. I have a feeling she might find her way again, though."

"We all lose our way from time to time," the bishop said, eyeing Ruth. "The main thing is finding our way back." He nodded to Ruth. "Let me get back to my wife."

The *Englischer* who brought Ruth's supply of wood for the winter joined her and Albert. "My condolences, Ms. Raber. Your mother was a special lady to just about everyone around these parts. She comforted many a person with one of her quilts. She even gave me one."

"My folks had one too," Albert said. "They loved sitting on the sofa with it over their legs while they watched TV."

"Lots of people have similar stories," the wood man said. Ruth started to ask his name but didn't see the need. He nodded to Albert and her. "I think I'll try a slice of that shoo-fly pie and head home."

"Not a bad idea," Albert said. He faced Ruth. "Maybe I'll see you around town sometime. Take care."

As Ruth watched him leave, not only could she feel the stares of everyone in the room, she could hear their thoughts: *Look at her speaking to those men. Even at her age, no sooner than her Mamm is in the grave, she tries to find a husband when she couldn't find one as a young woman—an Englisch husband at that. Oh, no, that one man takes her wood. It's the other one she likes. I saw them on the road when he came back from the war. I saw them too, walking down her driveway. Both are sinners if you ask me, especially her, being Amish.*

Nausea filled Ruth's throat. She left the glass on the window sill and dumped the plate in the trash. Donning her coat and bonnet, she splashed through the cemetery.

Three men had finished covering *Mamm's* coffin and were loading their shovels into buggies. They went inside, likely to enjoy a meal.

At the muddy mound of soil, Ruth stopped. Thank *Gott* the rain had slowed to a mist again. She needed to get something off her chest and didn't care to get soaked. "I suppose you're happy in Heaven now, *Mamm* and *Daed*. You don't have to see my plain face now, and I won't shame you by not finding a husband or having children and grandchildren. Regardless of your cruelty to me, I did my duty of caring for you both."

She paused. More words trembled on her lips. "I loved you both but you didn't love me," she said, her voice edged with tears. "If you did, you wouldn't have said I was too plain to find a husband. Those words scarred me like a knife to my heart. I was happy before then. I was starting to get over what Timothy said about me resembling a pig, but it all changed when you said I was plain."

Tears flowed down Ruth's cheeks. She had thought her words might make her feel better, but they only emptied her soul even more, as if it had never existed.

She touched the curved top of *Daed's* headstone. The coarse stone felt like the sandpaper he used to smooth his woodworking projects with, except it was wet from the rain.

You scolding your parents didn't work out

like you thought it would, did it? the booming voice asked. *It's not their fault you feel like you do. It's not Timothy's fault either.*

Ruth pressed her hands over her ears. She had hoped to have heard the last of the booming voice in her mind.

Cover your ears all you want. You know who made the decision to feel like you do. The voice chuckled. *Don't worry, I'll leave you for now. Just remember this—you cannot leave yourself.*

Chapter 6

Ruth raised her head. She had slid from the rocking chair to her knees, which pained her from striking the wood floor. Her face had pressed into *Mamm's* bed. Her tears had wet the quilt. Her eyes ached from crying.

Pushing up from the bed with her hands, she rose. The best way to forget these despicable memories was to start her day, and she would do that by caring for the animals and bringing more wood to the porch.

In the kitchen, she decided to warm a biscuit and have coffee. When she went to the icebox, it was empty. When she checked her supply of coffee, it was gone. She whirled from the cupboard to search the room. Frost glittered on the tables, on the walls, even on the wood cookstove. Her breath clouded and dissipated, clouded and dissipated.

She donned her coat and crunched through the snow to the barn. The aromas of hay and decades old manure assaulted her sense of smell. The stalls were empty — no horse, no cow.

Outside, she peered into the henhouse. No hens. No Big Red.

Behind the barn, no wood waited to warm the kitchen.

Stumbling to the house, her heart thudding, her breath hitching, her throat burning from the icy air, she collapsed to the snow and rolled over. Above her, the sky churned with spiraling clouds, white and intense. Blue peeked from between them, then turned black as night.

The ground shook with a sound like

thunder. To her left and right, huge holes appeared. Flames burst from them—flames and smoke and the smell of what might be brimstone. Two hands extended from the holes. The flesh burned away to reveal claws of bone. *It's time,* she thought. *I've died and have been lying here for who knows how long, and now I must answer for my sins.*

The claws curled toward her. A wicked laugh resounded from beneath her.

But what sins had she committed? Maybe she wasn't dead and could repent? Maybe it wasn't too late?

Gott, please have mercy and make my mind clear. Tell me what sins I have committed so I can repent.

The claws came closer. The laugh grew louder. The cracked fingernails scraped her face.

Gott! Heavenly Father! Please have mer—

Chapter 7

In town, on one of the wooden benches in the aisle of the hardware store, Albert nodded toward the bishop as he sat. "Morning, Bishop. It's mighty cold out."

The bishop leaned close to the stove and rubbed his hands together. "As cold as I've ever felt, Albert."

"Do you want to wait for Ed? I imagine he's hauling wood to chilly customers this morning."

Over the door, the brass bell rang to announce Ed Elliot. On the way to the bench opposite Albert's bench, his work boots clomped the hardwood floor. Like the bishop, he sat and leaned close to the stove to rub his hands together. "Morning, gents. The thermometer said eight degrees at sunrise. My old pickup moaned and groaned, but she started for me."

Albert chuckled. "I know how your truck feels. I turned eighty last week, and I think the good Lord let me live this long to teach Ruth a lesson. I met her twenty years ago. I sure thought she would've figured things out by now."

"A lot of people thought the same thing over the years," Ed said. "I've been selling her wood for over fifty years. Never had a customer as grouchy as her. Most invite me in for coffee. She just ignores my hints."

"Which leads us to the subject." The bishop set his hat on the bench and ran his fingers through his gray hair. "Have you men told everyone in town about our plan? I've told all the Amish and Mennonites."

"I told all my customers," Ed said.

Albert touched the tips of his right thumb and index finger together for the "OK" sign and raised it in the air. "I've told everyone I know. Myrna at the Post Office said the same, so that should be everyone. I also made sure Ruth's brother knows."

"I hope it goes well," Ed said.

"Me too," the bishop said. "Over the years, myself and plenty of other people have tried to get Ruth involved in life again. I don't know why she prefers to stay cooped up in that house. The last time I tried was on the day of her *mamm's* funeral. She wouldn't even entertain the thought."

Albert rubbed his chin. "I suppose it's up to me and my powers of persuasion. I told you both how she and I met when I came back from the war. The poor thing was starved for affection. You'd think a person of sixty would have more confidence than that."

"Especially an Amish person," Ed said.

The bishop cut his eyes at Ed. "We're all *Gott's* children, Ed. We have the same flesh and blood, the same feelings and the same faults. Faith helps us recognize those faults. It helps us know we can overcome them because He lives in our hearts."

"Amen to that," Albert said.

"I agree," Ed said. "What I don't understand about Ms. Raber is how she could have such a kind mother and end up so crotchety. That woman must've given away hundreds of quilts over the years. I have yet to hear a single person say the one they received wasn't a blessing in one way or another." He paused to look away. Albert watched him finger a tear from his eye. Ed cleared his throat and faced them again. "Sorry about that."

The bishop reached over to pat his hand. "Don't be sorry, Ed. We know you miss Mary."

Albert stood. "All right. If we're in agreement with our plan, it'll happen Christmas Eve at five in the afternoon tomorrow." He patted his stomach. "I assume we'll have plenty of food, right?"

"Darn tootin', Ed said. "All the ladies round here sure know how to cook."

"My wife's working on it now," the bishop said.

He and Ed stood. Each man shook hands with the other.

In Albert's pickup, as he drove to the town community center to make sure they had enough tables and chairs, he whistled the nameless tune he and Ruth had danced to so many years ago. "Well, Ruth, I'll be seeing you tomorrow afternoon at five. Don't let me down by refusing me. I'd hate to have to carry you to my pickup to make you go, but I'll do it if I have to."

Chapter 8

About to scream from the touch of those cracked fingernails scraping her cheeks, Ruth opened her eyes. She was still kneeling by *Mamm's* bed, both the quilt and her face still wet with tears.

She eased into the chair, gasping at the first memory she had never experienced.

Or had it been real?

She donned her coat and bonnet and rushed outside as fast as her trembling legs and the deep snow would allow her. In the barn, the horse and cow stared as if to ask, "Where's my food, old woman?" In the henhouse, the hens sitting on their nests did the same. Big Red cocked his head to one side and aimed a peck at Ruth's shin, but she stepped backward into the sunlight and closed the door in his face. Behind the barn, she verified plenty of wood beneath the tarp. Satisfied, she went back into the house, where she dropped into the rocking chair by the wood stove and held the Bible to her chest.

Since she had been having this series of memories again, she had wondered if she were dying, either from her heart, a stroke, or from the black spot on her nose that might be cancer. She had also thought she might die in the yard and not be found until spring, when the snow covering her body melted. Could the last scene she had just experienced be a warning about her faith? She pressed the Bible harder to her chest. Or was that scene a warning because of her *lack* of faith? How could that be when she had vowed to follow her community's *Ordnung,* when she read the Bible every single day, when she prayed almost constantly?

Ruth listened intently for the small, still voice that people said they heard when *Gott* was speaking to them.

No answer came.

Nothing.

She placed the Bible on the table beside her, said a quick prayer for understanding, and rose from the chair like she had for the last several decades, to start her day. Work was a blessing. Surely *Gott* would send her an answer while she worked. After all, her ordeal at *Mamm's* bedside had made her forget to feed and water the animals.

Outside again, she enjoyed the rising sun warming the black bonnet on her head. The light reflected off the snow. Glaring into her eyes, it reminded her of the song, *I Saw the Light.* The thought set her to humming. The humming set her to quickening her step in the snow, now turning to slush.

The hens and Big Red happily pecked at the grain she fed them, bought at the hardware store in town. Then they dipped their beaks into their water tray and raised them to let their sips drizzle down their throats.

In the barn, Ruth remembered the horse's name. "Good morning, Lucy," she said, rubbing the long neck. Lucy enjoyed her hay and oats and water as much as the chickens did their food.

At the cow's stall, Ruth tapped a finger to her chin. "I ought to name you, old girl. How about Lulu?" The cow raised her head from the hay; brown stems hung from the working lips. Ruth nodded. "Lulu it is."

She didn't understand her lighthearted attitude. Not an hour ago, she had thought she was about die and be snatched into the underworld. Now, for some reason, she felt as if the warming day was creating a warming heart within her chest.

About to leave the barn, she stopped to watch a shaft of sunlight beam to the dirt floor through a space between two boards. No, her heart wasn't warming from the sun.

Like in *Mamm's* bedroom, a single dust mote brightened inside the beam of sunlight. If Ruth didn't know any better, and she didn't, those brightening dust motes were a sign of something inside her—perhaps a hint, perhaps not—of some kind of sign. The trick was to recognize that sign, and she had the feeling she might miss it if she didn't continue to listen for the still, small voice.

The dust mote brightened again, reminding her of the first time she saw a firefly, when she was four or five and Timothy was three or four.

Mamm and *Daed* loved to sit on the porch after supper on summer nights and let her and Timothy run and laugh until dusk, their bare feet wet in the dew-soaked grass. The two rocking chairs *Daed* made would creak. His and *Mamm's* voices, soft and low, carried love and hopes for their children. As the shadows lengthened and the crickets chirped into soothing song, as the last breath of the day stirred the leaves on the oak, maple, and hickory trees in the woods bordering the yard, as the whippoorwills called to one another from across the fields, Ruth's first firefly winked into view amongst the darkening tree trunks.

She ran to the porch and pointed toward the woods. "What's that?"

Daed scooped her into his lap. "It's a firefly, Ruth."

"If you watch," *Mamm* said, "another one will light, then another and another."

Timothy came and crawled into *Mamm's* lap, and they all sat silently as the darkening woods came to life with tiny, blinking points of light.

Daed hugged Ruth tight. His clothes smelled of sunshine and hard work. "Those fireflies are like people. We can point the way with the light of *Gott's* word through our faith. Above all, we must have faith in Him because He has faith in us. We will fail Him, but He forgives us because He knows we're human and we're too weak to never sin. You've got to have faith, though."

Mamm sighed in agreement. "Listen to your *Daed*, Ruth. There will be times in your life when you'll doubt yourself. *Gott* never doubts you, so don't you do it either. If you can remember that, your troubles will slide off your back like water off a duck's feathers. If not, it will stick to you as if you were a porcupine, and that load of troubles will grow and grow until you can no longer bear the load. Then you'll become hard-hearted and unkind, and that is a sad thing indeed."

Ruth hadn't remembered that evening in years. She smiled at it, then wept bitterly, leaning her head against a post in the barn. How could she have had such a perfect childhood and the rest of her life turn out so badly?

In the driveway, a horse whinnied, followed by the rhythmic note of its hooves splashing in the melting snow. She opened the barn door to see Timothy climbing down from his open buggy. He went to Ruth for a quick huh. "Merry Christmas, *schweschder*. The day after tomorrow is the big day, is it not?"

For some reason Ruth didn't understand, she enjoyed the hug. "Why it is, isn't it?"

"Do you need anything from town tomorrow? I have to run by there for some flour and sugar for Anna around five, so I can get something for you if you'd like."

Ruth tilted her head to one side. "Why are you waiting until five?"

"Um ... well, I need to do a few things around the house first."

"You just came through town to get here. Can't you get whatever you need on the way back home?"

"Maybe I'm making an excuse to bring you a present. Isn't that all right?"

Ruth shrugged. "I suppose so, not that I need anything."

Timothy grinned. "Well, we're making

sure you get something whether you need it or not, but I think you need it."

Ruth straightened her head. "What do you mean 'we'?"

"It's … uh, it's just a figure of speech."

"You can bring me a bag of coffee and a gallon of milk. I should sell Lulu. She hasn't given milk in years, but she's good company for Lucy."

"Ah," Timothy said with a grin, "you finally named the cow." He paused to study her, his eyes narrowing. "You look a little different." He playfully patted her shoulder. "You don't have a boyfriend, do you?"

Ruth did something for her *bruder* she hadn't done since before he said she resembled a pig: she smiled warmly at him. "I'm too old for that nonsense." She returned the pat to his shoulder. "Maybe it's this warming day. I feel like my cold old heart is thawing along with the snow." She took in a breath of the chilly air, clean and fresh. "Ah, this air smells wonderful."

Timothy Took a deep breath too. "I agree. It makes me feel like a new man."

"Or in my case," Ruth said, "a new woman." The comment surprised her, as if a spark had been kindled in her heart, possibly like the glowing dust mote in *Mamm's* room and in the barn a moment ago.

Saying he would see her tomorrow, Timothy climbed into the buggy and left for the main road, his hand out to one side waving.

Taking advantage of the easier walk through the quickly melting snow, Ruth piled wood on the porch. Satisfied, she went inside for coffee. Before she poured it, she went to Timothy's old room. Only the bed remained. He had taken the dresser and chest of drawers when he got married. One of *Mamm's* Wedding Ring quilts covered the mattress and the single pillow. She went to it and patted it, affectionately remembering the pillow fight when *Daed* came in and said he was happy to see them happy.

Ruth's knees buckled. Tears burned her eyes.

That's right, the booming voice said. *You remember what you almost did to your brother on the night he first said you resembled a pig.*

Ruth gasped. Her chest heaved. "I was a child. I … I didn't know any better."

He was a child too, so why have you held his childish words against him for most of your life? You stood there with your own pillow, ready to smother him because of a childish comment, and you only now remember it. I wonder why that is, Ruth? Do you hear that still, small voice yet?

Weeping bitterly, Ruth pressed her face into the quilt. Between sobs and coughs, she pressed her hands together and looked to the Heavens. "*Gott,* please forgive me," she wailed. "I was only a child."

The booming voice said nothing. No still, small voice spoke. The clean feeling she had felt moments earlier was replaced with grief. She went to *Daed* and *Mamm's* bed. Again she knelt to press her hands together and look toward the Heavens. *"Daed, Mamm,* please forgive me. I'm sorry for being unkind. I was just a child, I didn't know any better."

No one answered. No one forgave her.

Not even *Gott.*

She wept bitterly, even until her throat grew raw and her eyes felt as if they would burst from their sockets.

Her vision of those claws reaching for her could only mean one thing: because of her sins, she was bound for fire and brimstone, and she didn't even know why. Her vows to follow her community's *Ordnung* were worthless. Reading the Bible over and over again was worthless.

The remainder of the day passed with pouring from the coffeepot while sitting in the rocking chair by the wood stove, with glances at the Bible on the table by the chair every so often.

Emptiness engulfed Ruth. The chair could be in the middle of a field covered with blinding white snow—no trees, no houses, no animals, no nothing—and she wouldn't be any more alone than she felt now.

She ate nothing for supper. Dusk fell. Darkness filled the windows. She refused to light the lamp beside her. Two tiny eyes of orange light peered at her from two spaces near the hinges of the wood stove. The fire cracked and popped.

The night grew cold. In bed, the sheets chilled her from head to toe. An occasional pair of headlights passed on the road. Closed eyes refused sleep. A heavy heart refused to pray. A sinful soul refused to rest.

Ruth wept.

Chapter 9

Ruth woke to more aches and pains than she had ever felt in her life. She managed to dress without groaning too much from her stiff back, but pinning her hair with her swollen arthritic fingers was the chore of all chores. Bending over to tie her shoes was impossible, so she slipped them on and went to the kitchen to prop them in a chair one at the time to tie them. Next came stoking the wood stove and making coffee, which she cooled by blowing between sips.

She had slept late, evidenced by the sun in the window and Big Red crowing as if he intended to squawk his gizzard out. Of course, as always, Lucy was whinnying and Lulu was mooing. Still, they were the only company Ruth had even now, on Christmas Eve.

On the porch, she paused at the warmth of the day, a gift from *Gott,* no doubt. Most of the snow had melted, leaving a few piles of slush scattered about the yard.

As she cared for the animals, she considered the young men she was interested in during her younger years. The last she heard, before she stopped attending church, Thomas Yoder and Susan Stoltzfus had two children. They and any others would be grown with their own children by now. Ethan Peachy, the boy at the orchard, was married too. He now ran the orchard, inherited from his *Daed,* and also had children.

Ruth tried to imagine the life she could've treasured if one of those boys had given her a chance. Actually, as she thought about them further, she hadn't given Ethan a chance at all, despite his interest in her. For Thomas, she never knew if he had been interested in her or not. Probably not, since he had hopped up from the singing bench and sat across from Susan without a single word.

Then there was Albert, the older gentleman she had met when he was returning from the Korean War. Of all the men she had met, he had intrigued her the most. The fact that he was *Englisch* hadn't bothered her one bit, and she didn't understand it one bit either. Weren't the Amish supposed to set themselves apart from the *Englisch* in order to not be influenced by their prideful ways?

The lack of an answer frustrated Ruth. Albert said he had accepted *Gott*. Wasn't that, regardless of the person being Amish, Mennonite, *Englisch*, or whoever, the important thing? After all, faith was faith, and her faith—

Ruth's throat spasmed shut. *Her* faith?

Her faith? If her faith had been as strong as she had thought it was, why had her life been so lonely?

Then she remembered how she had considered smothering her own *bruder*, and how her vows to her community's *Ordnung* were worthless. If that were true, her faith might be worthless too.

The revelation stopped her halfway up the porch steps, where she dropped down to sit. The angle of the sun said she had worked well past noon. What had Timothy said about stopping by? The sun warmed her black bonnet. Despite her hunger from not having supper last night, or breakfast or lunch today, she leaned her head against the porch post and closed her eyes, feeling like an old hound dog they once had that loved sleeping on the porch in the sun.

Ruth released her conscious mind into a drowsy half-sleep. She used to do this as a girl, upset about her nose and her plain features, which allowed her a few minutes of escape during chores.

Colors swirled in her mind, forming and reforming into childhood memories, both happy and sad. These memories then changed into teenage recollections, such as when Thomas Yoder and Ethan Peachy had rejected her. Albert appeared next as they danced in the barn over twenty years ago.

A pair of weights pressed on Ruth's thighs. The weights transformed into two children. On her left thigh, a boy with blond curls held her hand. "Please tell us the Christmas story from Luke."

"Oh, please do," the girl said, peering up with sky-blue eyes.

The boy giggled. "Can you make the sounds of the sheep and the donkeys in the stable? It makes it so real."

Ruth wondered who these children were. Perhaps, if she had married, they would've been hers.

The children shimmered into billions of brilliant dust motes and swirled upward in a spiral to fade away. The faces of the men and boys faded also. *Mamm* sat at the table sewing a quilt. Timothy sat in *Daed's* lap as he read the story of the birth of Christ in Luke. A wreath of running cedar decorated the fireplace mantle, so it was Christmas. Funny how Ruth used the wood stove for heat instead of the fireplace, almost as if she were trying to purge her mind of the time when she refused to climb into *Daed's* lap while he read to Timothy.

Cheerfully, the split oak in the fireplace burned with multicolored flames. A knot popped. Mixed with smoke, sparks flew up the chimney.

Mamm called Ruth to the table. "Did I ever tell you why I make all my quilts into Wedding Ring quilts?"

Ruth told *Mamm* the part about circles meaning the continuation of love in a marriage, and the love *Gott* means for marriage to be, like the love Jesus has for us all.

"That's true," Mamm said, softly smiling, "but there's another reason I make them. You see, forgiveness is a circle too. When we repent—I mean *truly* repent, not just say we repent—*Gott* forgives us. Even then, though, we sometimes can't seem to forgive ourselves. When that happens, it separates us from His plan for us in life ... separates us from His plan for us in life ... separates us from His plan for us in li—"

A vehicle engine woke Ruth. She opened her eyes to see a man pulling up to the house in a pickup truck. He opened the door and climbed out. His iron-gray hair was receding from his high forehead. Crow's feet lined the corners of his eyes. He wore blue denims, black dress shoes, a suit jacket, and a white shirt with one button loose at the throat. Nearing the porch, he removed a narrow-brimmed hat like the *Englisch* wore to church, a black satin band around its base. For a moment he smiled. "Why, hello, Ruth. It's been a long time, hasn't it? I guess you don't recognize me."

Looking up from the black tunnel of her bonnet, she shaded her eyes from the sun. "You're not that *Englischer* who brings the wood."

The man chuckled. "His name is Ed. He's a good friend of mine. Of a lot of people."

That voice, Ruth thought. She tried to stand. The man took her hand and helped her up. He then hummed a tune. "Does that help, Ruth?"

Her mouth gaped. "Albert? Is it really you?"

He chuckled again. "It sure is. I'm a little older and a lot wiser. It's good to see you. What's the chance I can take you to dinner in town. I did ask you that back when we met, you know."

Ruth asked him the time. He pulled his suit coat sleeve back and told her it was quarter to five.

"I should stay. My *bruder* is stopping by." Her shoes were muddy from tramping in the yard. Her dress was dirty from carrying wood. The sour smell of body odor rose from her armpits. "I'm not decent either."

Albert removed his hat. "I can wait while you get ready. As far as Timothy, we're good friends too. I'm sure he won't mind missing you. We can leave a note if you'd like."

We, Ruth thought. *How long have I wanted to be a we instead of a me?* "Well, let's go in. I'll change as fast as I can."

She left Albert sitting at the kitchen table. At the basin in her bedroom, feeling like a young woman again, she washed under her arms, re-pinned her hair, and donned a clean black dress and shoes. Then she added a clean white kapp, a bonnet, and a shawl for the drive back later, when it would be colder.

"Ah, don't you look fine," Albert said when she entered the kitchen. "Let's hit the road, shall we?"

Ruth wrote a note and stuck it in the

screened door when she closed it. "Yes, Albert. Let's—as you say—hit the road."

During the drive, question after question ran through Ruth's mind, but the main one was why Albert hadn't visited before now? She glanced at him, and the question didn't matter. What mattered was this moment, this feeling, this *amazing* feeling. What might compare to it, she had no idea, even at her advanced age. Here she was, eighty years old, going out on her first date with a handsome man. That he was *Englisch* didn't matter one whit, or did it?

"Since you know Ed and Timothy," she asked, "do you know Bishop Dickens too?"

"I sure do. Charley and I go way back."

"I heard his wife call him Charles."

"We might see him." Albert winked at Ruth. "Try calling him Charlie. He won't mind."

In town, strung from light poles, red and green lights made Ruth point. She had avoided town during Christmas all her life and wondered what the lights were for. "What are those lights for?" she asked Albert.

"They're decorations for Christmas," he said. "I take it you don't come to town during Christmas."

"Not really. I'm uncomfortable around crowds."

Inside all the stores—the hardware, the grocery, the department store, the drug store—red and green lights lined the windows. Some kind of white material that resembled snow covered the lower section of each window. The town sure enjoyed decorating for Christmas when the Amish tried to not overdo. In the department store, Ruth thought she saw an evergreen tree with red and green lights twinkling along its branches. If she saw a tree like that as a child, she didn't remember. Maybe it was some kind of new fad.

Albert left town. A minute or so later, he parked in a lot at a huge building with a sign out front that said Christiansburg Community Center. Both Amish buggies and *Englisch* cars and pickup trucks filled the lot. Ruth faced him. "I thought we were going to eat supper?"

"We are." Albert put his hat on. "The town is having its annual Christmas gathering, and there'll be plenty of food here." He opened the pickup door but Ruth didn't open hers. "Come on now, Ruth. It'll be fine. I promise."

"I'm not sure."

"Do you trust me?"

"Well …"

"Aren't you hungry? You looked like you had been working all day when I saw you at your house."

Ruth's stomach rumbled from eating almost nothing since yesterday. She climbed from the truck and met Albert at its front bumper. "Just who all is here?"

"Amish, Mennonites, all the town people."

Without meaning to, Ruth twisted her lips to one side in a disgusted frown. She would go in long enough to eat and then make Albert take her home. If he refused, or if anyone was unkind to her, she would walk. Albert offered his hand. "Come now, fair lady. Let's go in and say hello."

He helped her up the steps and held the door while she entered. Adults and children of all ages, all wearing an amazing mix of Amish, Mennonite, and *Englisch* clothing, filled the building. The *Englisch* men wore clothes similar to Albert, except some wore dress slacks. They wore their hair short, some slicked back, some combed to one side. The *Englisch* women wore dresses in red, green, and blue that flared at the knee and were conservative at the neckline. Some wore broaches that resembled Christmas wreathes, small brass bells, or tiny signs that read Merry Christmas! Many wore necklaces with gold crosses. Most wore high heel shoes and pink or red lipstick that enhanced their vivid smiles.

No one smoked, likely out of respect for everyone in the building, which was exceedingly thoughtful.

The Old Order Amish men wore black pants and suspenders over white shirts with hook-and-eye closures. A beard signified marriage. Their haircuts resembled umbrellas down to their ears. Amongst them, smiles were the order of the day also.

The Old Order Amish women, of course, were dressed exactly like Ruth, all in black except for their white prayer kapps, while most of the Mennonite women wore dresses of blue, their hair covered with a white prayer kapps as well. Not a single Amish or Mennonite person appeared uncomfortable around the *Englisch*. In fact, they talked and smiled and laughed like old friends.

To the right of the door, several tables in a row held all kinds of food, from roasted and fried chicken, to savory soups, to broiled beef and pork roasts, to every vegetable a garden would grow, to casserole after casserole. Ruth's mouth started watering, but when she saw the last table, filled with pies, cookies, cakes, and puddings, she had to swallow her saliva.

A hand fell on her shoulder and eased her around. Timothy hugged her. "Merry Christmas, *schweschder.*"

Anna joined them. "We're so happy you came, Ruth." She gestured across the room. All our children are here with their children." She waved toward a young woman with a bundle in her arms.

She came over and focused her dark brown eyes on Ruth. "Merry Christmas, Aunt Ruth."

Ann uncovered the top end of the bundle, revealing a beautiful baby. "Meet Ruth, our first great-grandchild."

Ruth blinked. "You named her Ruth?"

"Because of her cute nose like yours," Timothy said.

Before Ruth could respond, the wood

man—Ed—came over. "Look who's here, my favorite customer." Grinning, he elbowed Albert. "Ruth pays me for the heat of my wood with the smell of her coffee."

A flash of embarrassment warmed Ruth's cheeks. Ed was right. In all the years he had delivered her wood, she had never invited him in for coffee. "I apologize, Ed. I have no excuse for being so unkind."

Ed chuckled. "Don't give it another thought."

Albert pointed to a corner of the room. "That's quite the Christmas tree. I cut it on my farm. Have you ever seen one?"

Ruth said she hadn't, but she thought it was too much decoration for such an important day. "I suppose the boxes underneath are presents. We wrap ours with brown paper. What does the star on top mean?"

"It represents the star over the manger scene in Luke," Albert said. "I thought sure you'd know that."

"I haven't read Luke in years. *Daed* used to read it before … well … before he left us. I once could recall it word for word. I don't remember the first one now."

From near a fireplace, at the center of the far wall, where logs burned cheerfully, Bishop Dickens clapped his hands. "Good evening, everyone. Welcome to our annual Christmas gathering. I'm sure we're all ready to eat, but I'd like to have someone come up and take a seat by the fire first. As you all know, we've been planning this for some time because of our love for our *schweschder*." He waved Ruth over. "Ruth, please come and have a seat. Most everyone here would like to share something with you."

Ruth swallowed hard. As well as not liking large crowds, she didn't like being the center of attention. "Please," she said, "I'm not important, Bishop. Just say the blessing so everyone can eat."

Albert leaned close to her ear and

whispered, "You can either take a seat, or we can show all these fine people how to dance. What will it be?"

Shaking her head, she let him lead her to a single rocking chair to the right of the fireplace and sat. He sat on a bench at a nearby table, where Timothy and Anna and their family sat.

The bishop nodded toward Ed, standing beside him. Ed hurried outside and came back with a folded quilt. He came to stand before Ruth. "Ms. Raber, your mother gave me this quilt years ago. Of all the quilts my wife owned, it was her favorite. I lost her to cancer last year. She would lie in bed and run her fingers over those wedding rings and say how much comfort the kindness of your mother gave her." He paused to finger a tear from one eye. "I just wanted to let you know." He gave Ruth a quick hug and went to stand by the bishop.

Albert went outside and came back with a quilt. Like Ed, he stood before Ruth.

"Ruth, your mother gave my mother this quilt years ago. She knelt by the bed with her elbows on it every night and prayed for my safe return. She said your mother's kindness comforted her during all the long hours she prayed for me." He hugged her and returned to the bench.

Person after person, either Amish, Mennonite, or *Englisch,* shared similar stories of how *Maam's* kindness had comforted them, including, to Ruth's surprise, Ethan Peachy, who said his wife had given birth to their first child one winter while their quilt had kept her warm.

When he was done, the bishop asked if there were any more people who wanted to share their experiences with one of *Mamm's* quilts. Everyone glanced around.

From within the crowd, using a cane, an elderly Amish man hobbled to Ruth, a folded quilt beneath his arm. A woman, his wife Ruth assumed, came with him. They stopped before Ruth. "I'm Thomas Yoder," he said.

"And this is Susan, your wife," Ruth said. "It's nice to see you again."

Thomas smiled, revealing false teeth. "I hope you forgive me for jumping up from that singing bench so long ago. I was going to stay until I remembered I had promised to sing with Susan. I should've told you, and I'm sorry I didn't."

Susan faced Ruth. "We Amish usually don't talk about such things, but I'm going to. We lost our third child in a miscarriage. We couldn't have any more children after that, so the doctor said. We buried our sweet Nora with the quilt your *mamm* gave us, and it comforted us that she was wrapped in so much kindness."

One after the other, they hugged Ruth, whose eyes burned with tears. Every quilt *Mamm* had given these people with unending kindness had comforted them in one way or another, and all she had ever done was to be unkind, and she didn't even know why?

Or did she?

She rose from the chair. "You all have touched my heart tonight. Please go ahead and eat. I need Albert to run me home for something." Several people asked her to stay and eat, saying she could go home after, but Ruth insisted, adding, "Don't you worry. The smell of all that food will bring me back, or my name isn't Ruth Raber."

As lines formed at the tables, Albert helped her out and into his pickup. Once they were on the road, he faced her. You were crying while ago, Ruth. Are you all right?"

Ruth took a handkerchief from her dress pocket and wiped her eyes. "I'm ashamed, is what I am. I've led a lonely life when I could've had a town full of friends because of my *Mamm's* kindness." She paused. "And *Daed's* kindness too. There's no telling how much cloth and thread he bought over the years for *Mamm* to make those quilts, and I never heard him say a word against it."

"Ah," Albert said.

Ruth said nothing until he parked at her house and they went inside. "Have a seat if you'd like. I'll be back in a few minutes."

In *Mamm's* room, she opened each drawer in the chest of drawers and in the dresser. Every drawer held all the quilts *Mamm* had sewn after her strokes. One by one she lay them on the bed, intending to take them back to the community center and return the gifts of love those people had given her.

In the bottom drawer of the dresser, when she took the last quilt out, a folded piece of paper beneath it caught her eye. She took it out to read. Upon comprehending the first words—*Dear Ruth, from Daed, Mamm, and Timothy*—she dropped to the bed, legs trembling, hands shaking. After taking a match from the nightstand drawer, she lit the lamp, perched a pair of *Mamm's* reading glasses on her nose, and continued reading.

For years we've prayed for you to find your way in life. Although the values of our Ordnung are of family, community, and of kindness to one another, the most important value is kindness. A person doesn't need to marry to be kind, so that's not what this letter is about.

We know you have kindness in you, but something is holding it back. Of course, your bruder doesn't know you as your daed and I know you. Saying that, we don't know you as Gott knows you.

You see, Ruth, even though you took your vows to the church and our Ordnung, and even though you read the Bible and pray, we're afraid you don't know Gott as you should. If you did, your kindness would shine through, and it doesn't.

As in everything we and Gott do for you, this isn't a criticism. We tell you this because people are meant for a full life, and they cannot have that if they separate themselves from Gott.

As those words sank into Ruth's mind, more took their place, words from both *Mamm* and *Daed:*

"Forgiveness is a circle too," *Mamm* said. "When we repent—I mean truly repent, not just say we repent—*Gott* forgives us. Even then, though, we sometimes can't seem to forgive ourselves. When that happens, it separates us from His plan for us in life."

"For we are the children of *Gott,*" *Daed* said from his death bed, his hands resting on the quilt, "with lives to live as He would have us live, with kindness never-ending, a circle from beginning to end, returned to us in kind—kindness to kindness to kindness everlasting."

As Ruth pondered their meaning, more words—words from an unexpected person—came to her:

"I had let some teasing boy bother me," Albert said, "even to the point of ruining my faith and not finding a special lady to love because I was so shy."

The meaning of *Mamm's* letter and Albert's words from that day in the barn struck Ruth with a force she had never felt, as if the Lord Himself had taken hold of her shoulders and had shaken her.

Despite her claims of taking her vows, or of reading the Bible, or of constantly praying, she was a sinner. Worse than that, she didn't know *Gott*. Even worse than that, her lack of faith had allowed Timothy's teasing about her resembling a pig to ruin the faith in herself that *Gott* had in her. Then, when *Daed* and *Mamm* said she might be too plain to find a husband, it happened all over again, but worse, like the final nail in the coffin lid hiding her faith.

The night Ruth saw her first fireflies hovered before her.

Daed hugged her tight. His clothes smelled of sunshine and hard work. "Those fireflies are like people. We can point the way with the light of *Gott's* word through our faith. Above all, we must have faith in

Him because He has faith in us. We will fail Him, but He forgives us because He knows we're human and we're too weak to never sin. You've got to have faith, though."

Mamm sighed in agreement. "Listen to your *Daed*, Ruth. There will be times in your life when you'll doubt yourself. *Gott* never doubts you, so don't you do it either. If you can remember that, your troubles will slide off your back like water off a duck's feathers. If not, it will stick to you as if you were a porcupine, and that load of troubles will grow and grow until you can no longer bear the load. Then you'll become hard-hearted and unkind, and that is a sad thing indeed."

Through tears now, Ruth nodded. Because of her lack of faith, she had allowed *Daed* and *Mamm* and Timothy's words about her appearance to cling to her back as if she were a porcupine, weighing her entire life down until she couldn't bear the load. In turn, she had become unkind to a degree she had never heard of.

She returned to the letter:

So you see, Ruth, we're afraid you are separate from Gott. If you're reading this letter, it means one of two things. You are either throwing my quilts away, or your burden of sin has become too great to bear, and you are going to share these quilts like I did. We pray it is the latter. If so, our joy upon seeing you again in Heaven will be never ending. If so, consider this last quilt as a gift from us to you, your Forgiveness Quilt. Lay it across our bed. Place your hands together. Kneel down in reverence to Gott, Ruth, and accept Him into your heart.

Love always,

Daed, Maam, and Timothy.

Pressing the letter to her chest, Ruth wept and wept. Then, with a swipe of her handkerchief to her eyes, she stopped. "Now is not the time for regret," she announced. "Now, as the *Englisch* say, is the first day of the rest of my life." She knelt on the floor, placed her elbows on the Forgiveness Quilt, and pressed her palms together. "And I intend to make the most of it from this day forth."

Before she could close her eyes to pray, a searing pain gripped her heart, making her gasp and cry out. Then the pain turned cold instead of hot, then warm instead of cold, like a summer night with fireflies filling the woods with their winking, blinking lights.

Each and every pain Ruth felt left her. Her hazy eyesight cleared. The tears dried themselves.

And I shall wipe the tears from your eyes, the booming voice whispered.

Welcome home, Ruth.

Ruth stood on strengthened legs. No longer did she hunch over, for the weight of her burdens had left her. She kissed the letter, folded it and left it on the nightstand. "Thank you *Daed* and *Mamm.* I can't wait until I see you again. I'll hug you with all the love I can gather."

Albert knocked on the door. "Are you ok in there?"

Ruth opened the door. "I'm sorry to ask, but can you help me take all these quilts to your truck? I'd like to continue my *Mamm's* tradition of making them and giving them as gifts."

Albert smiled broadly, then winked. "I do believe a certain young lady has had an epiphany."

"Oh poo," she said, playfully slapping his arm. "Stop all your teasing and help me with these quilts." She pointed to the one spread across the edge of the bed. "But not that one. That one stays here."

At the community center again, Ruth asked Albert to ask Timothy to help with the quilts. In no time at all, they were stacked to one side of the tree. Ruth faced the onlooking crowd, many of them still eating. "Can I have your attention please?" Several talking people quieted. The ones eating lowered either spoons or forks, and Ruth continued. "You have touched my heart with your stories about my *mamm's* quilts. She made all these under the tree after she had her first strokes, and I'd like to continue her tradition of making more and giving them away. If anyone wants to learn how, I'll be glad to show you in my home when I can make a schedule. Thank you so much for your kindness, and I apologize for being a hermit when I should've been a fine neighbor like you all have been." She licked her lips and rubbed her hands together. "Now *I* get to eat."

Timothy led her and Albert to a table. Four plates covered in foil waited for them. He removed the foil from two while Anna brought two glasses of lemonade. Each plate held a sample of most of the foods from the long tables. Timothy told them the other plates were samples of each dessert. Bishop Dickens came over and said a blessing, and Ruth and Albert picked up their forks.

Thought after thought ran through Ruth's mind while she ate. Some reminded her of the years she had wasted without faith, but each time she heard them, she reminded herself of the whispering voice of *Gott* saying, *And I shall wipe the tears from your eyes.* He had truly done so, and she was grateful beyond mere words.

After their meal, presents were passed out and opened. The Amish and Mennonites kept the tradition of giving simple gifts wrapped in brown paper. Many were hand-carved figures from the manger scene, created from soft pine by the men and given to the children. The ladies gave scarfs and candles and lovely needlepoint scenes, some of farms, some of the Bible, some of the manger scene, the Christmas Star burning brightly at the top.

The townspeople gave gifts wrapped in red, green, and gold paper tied with ribbons and bows of similar colors. Some presents were faceless dolls for Amish and Mennonite girls. Some were baseballs and bats for the boys. The girls and the boys from town received the same, but some received Bibles and New Testaments.

Ruth relaxed in the rocking chair by the fireplace. The embers glowed with warmth, similar to the warmth in her heart. Every few breaths she thanked *Gott* for his many, many blessings. Now, after all her years on earth, she knew what it felt like to be loved and accepted, and from people she didn't even know.

Albert had pulled one of the benches over to sit beside her. Like Ruth, the warmth of the fire and their full stomachs was making his eyes open and close, open and close.

Someone clapped their hands, startling them both. Beside Ruth, Bishop Dickens faced the crowd. "Is there a volunteer to read the story of Christ's birth in Luke?"

A boy and a girl ran up to Ruth, Ed following them. "These are my grandchildren, Ms. Raber. My wife used to read that story to them every Christmas Eve, and they were wondering if you would do the honors."

Happy tears filled Ruth's eyes. The children resembled the boy and girl in her dream, where she thought they were the children she might've had if she had married. She wiped her eyes. "I'll be happy to Ed, but you've got to promise me something first."

Ed frowned. "Well, I'll be glad to if you tell me what it is."

She patted her lap. "Set them up here and I'll tell you." He did, and she looked up into his questioning eyes. "Call me Ruth."

As the bishop offered her a Bible, Ruth shook her head. "No thank you, Charley. I remember every word."

The boy clapped his hands. "Don't forget to make the sounds."

"That's right," the girl said. "Grandma always made the sounds."

Ruth wrapped her arms around them both and settled back to rock the chair slowly. All around the room, everyone quieted until the only sounds were of their breathing.

"Eee-aw. Baa, baa," Ruth said, trying her best—through a grin—to sound like a donkey and a sheep. "All around the room, children giggled and adults smiled, holding them in their laps.

"'And it came to pass in those days," Ruth said, continuing the story that had been handed down from generation to generation about Christ's birth in a stable. She told the crowd why Joseph and Mary had traveled to Bethlehem, because of the decree from Caesar Augustus that all the world should be taxed. She told of the shepherds and how the angel of the Lord came upon them, saying on this day, in the city of David, a Savior, which is Christ the Lord has been born. She told how Mary wrapped him in swaddling clothes and laid him in a manger because there was no room for them in the inn.

At the end of the story. Ruth kissed the boy's blond curls and the girl's brown hair. They thanked her and hopped from her lap to return to Ed and his family.

Albert reached for Ruth's hand. "That was lovely, Ruth."

Bishop Dickens came over. "I heard that. "If you two would like to court, I have no objection. After all, as a bishop, I have the say so amongst my community."

Ruth burst out laughing. "Oh, stop your teasing, Charley. You're as bad as Albert."

Grinning, Charley chuckled. "Who's teasing? I happen to think you two are the perfect couple. Besides, you'll need help around the farm since you'll be teaching people to sew quilts."

Albert shrugged. "Us courting at our age, ain't that a hoot." He patted Ruth's hand. "I'm game if you are."

Ruth rolled her eyes at him. "I'll let you

know after our first date, when you take me out to supper like you promised twenty years ago."

Albert kissed her cheek. "You've got a deal, old girl." He stood from the bench. "Let me help everyone clean up so I can get you home."

Thomas Yoder left his wife, who was wrapping leftover food, and came over, his cane tapping the floor. "I enjoyed seeing you, Ruth."

"I enjoyed seeing you too, Thomas. I can't wait until next year."

"Next year?" Ethan Peachy asked from beside Ruth. "How about next Sunday, when you return to church?"

"An excellent idea," Timothy said, walking over. "I'll run by in the buggy to make sure you come."

Ruth agreed to their plan, and they all left to help clean up. Facing the glowing embers of the fire, she would've never imagined this day in her wildest dreams. Gratitude filled her to overflowing. Prayer after prayer of thanks and praise rose from her to *Gott*, to *Daed*, to *Mamm*. She could smell the air, fresh and crisp, of Heaven itself, could feel *Daed* and *Mamm's* arms around her, could hear them welcoming her home because of her faith, born to renew her like Jesus had been born to renew the world.

How many quilts would she sew before she left for Heaven? The number didn't matter, because the seed of faith had been sewn in her heart. With *Gott's* blessing, and with *Mamm and Daed's* blessing of the Forgiveness Quilt, that seed would continue to be sewn, sprouting anew in the hearts of the people who sewed them, who gave them, and who passed the tradition of love and kindness on and on and on, even until Jesus himself returned.

Ruth rose on steady feet and went to the Christmas tree. The star on top burned with brilliance. *Forgiveness is like that*, she thought. *It burns away the sadness and opens the heart to gladness.*

She thanked *Daed* for loving her despite her faults. She thanked *Gott* for believing in her when she didn't believe in herself.

She paused to sniff one of the tree's branches, which held the bright aroma of evergreen.

And she thanked *Mamm* for the Forgiveness Quilt, a blessing and a lesson she never expected, and which she would cherish for as long as she lived.

Dear reader,

Thank you for choosing this book. If you enjoyed reading it as much as I enjoyed writing it, you *really* enjoyed it. Saying that, please enjoy the first chapter of *Clara's Mourning,* the first book in what I call my Clara Engelman Series, to be published early in 2023. After this chapter, please enjoy the first chapter of *The Essence of Emmaline Strong.*

Thank you for reading.

Torn between admiration for the sunrise and the need to keep her memories of Abram tucked away like a chaste kiss, Clara didn't know whether to smile or cry. She had enjoyed similar scenes with him after they were married, but the one before her, nor the ones to come, would never compare. Still, the beauty of the breaking day was a gift from God, and it was worthy of her attention.

The shimmering line of crimson above the horizon lit the distant treetops with flame. The first air of dawn stirred, cold and brisk. In the chicken coop behind the barn, the rooster crowed. In the maple tree beside the single-story home clothed with white-painted boards, two bluebirds left their house attached to the trunk and fluttered to a limb to warble their waking song.

Clara's footsteps crunched in the greening grass. Her breath plumed before her face and dissipated as it shrouded her cheeks with white. She entered the dark kitchen and left the basket of eggs and the still illuminated flashlight on the table to light her way. For a moment she considered checking on Edna and John but didn't. Her footsteps, no matter how soft, might wake them if she approached their room, and they needed all the sleep they could get.

She paused for water. At the sink, sipping from the glass, she leaned closer to the window. Over the hill between her farm and the neighbor's farm, the rising sun etched the first rays of yellow into the sky. It was the first of April in southern Virginia, still capable of frost, and she had forgotten her mittens while gathering eggs, leaving her hands chilly from the morning cold.

She finished the water and went to the cookstove to add wood to the glowing embers. Leaving the cast iron door open, she pulled a chair over from the table and sat to warm her hands near the opening.

How she missed Abram's warm embraces in the nights, now long and lonely after his funeral a month ago. His death had left a hole in her life like a well without water: cold and damp, without the least bit of comfort. Four-year-old Edna and three-year-old John missed their papa as well, evidenced by the nightmares that still woke them at least three times a week. Thankfully, they had slept the last two nights without crying, nor asking when he would return from that terrible dark hole in the earth, now filled beneath the old oak tree behind the house.

Although she and Abram had been teaching them about their Heavenly home, they were too young to understand, much less understand about death. Regardless, Clara had tried to explain how living things died, using the example of a hen that had died of old age a few days after the funeral. All the children had managed was to look at her with huge, questioning eyes rimmed with tears.

The rooster crowed again, followed by more of the bluebird's warbling entering the screened door. She had left the wooden door open to remind her to milk the cow, one of the many chores that were now left to her alone.

Tears threatened. She attempted to blink them away.

Not only was she forced to endure life without Abram's love, she was forced to try to keep the farm profitable enough to feed her family and pay the bills.

Clara palmed the wetness from her eyes. How could she do all that without help? Not only had she never hitched the plow to their used tractor, she didn't know how to drive it, much less how to maintain it. At least she had two seasons of vegetables canned, so she and the children had plenty to eat, and the chickens would provide eggs and meat.

She bowed her head for a prayer of thanks for her Beachy Amish Mennonite brothers and sisters, who had built the coffin and helped with the funeral, and with bringing enough food so cooking hadn't been necessary for a week. She also appreciated their vows to continue helping, including with money, but it felt wrong to Clara to not earn her own way.

Even Bishop Silverman had calmed the children by saying all would be well, that their papa would never stop loving them and watching over them. If only Clara could've been comforted by those words.

Looking for a new area with large acreage for sale, plus being frugal with their meager funds, she and Abram had bought this farm. Tucked away in a somewhat isolated area in

Charlotte County, it was a late wedding gift to each other with the money his and her parents had given him. Unfortunately, her and Abram's parents lived in Pennsylvania, where their other children lived. Yes, they had made the drive for the funeral, but they had returned shortly after, saying they were needed back home.

Noting how the wood wasn't catching fire in the embers, Clara adjusted it with a poker until it flamed.

The smell of woodsmoke brought back the memory of her and Abram's first night here together, snug in several quilts in front of this very wood stove, the door open on a freezing January evening. Although they slept that way when it was bitterly cold, it was an adventure too, enjoyed in the early days of their marriage.

Rising from the chair, she shut the door and rose to get the pail for the milk. She considered the mittens on the shelf above the coat rack, but she wouldn't be able to roll her fingers properly as she milked, and the cow sometimes kicked if she felt something different.

Clara paused for another swallow of water. In the window over the sink, her reflection stared back. She'd risen and put on Abram's pants and wide-brimmed hat, both warmer than her dress and the bandana she tied over her hair while she worked. She'd also put on two pair of his socks and his work boots, leaving her looking nothing like the proper Beachy Amish housewife. Then again, the farm was over twenty miles away from the community she belonged to, a newer one north of the Amish community in Nathalie, Virginia, in Halifax County, so she wouldn't be caught out of her traditional clothing. Even if she were, she had arrived at the point of not caring, which she *didn't* care for.

Then again, she knew God loved her regardless, and His acceptance was more important than what others thought. Also, maybe she wore Abram's clothes to recall his warmth surrounding her, like a second skin of love she would never shed.

The two bluebirds continued to warble, and the sound saddened her. She and Abram used to call their nightly talks in bed talking like the bluebirds, when they spoke of the children and their dreams for them.

Clara refused to judge other religious beliefs, but she was grateful for her and Abram's Beachy Amish Mennonite Ordnung. Still, although a used pickup truck sat by the barn, she didn't know how to drive it. They had also discussed getting a telephone when they could afford it, which they couldn't yet. They hadn't minded living simply until they could do better, but how some of the stricter Amish lived without conveniences such as indoor plumbing, Clara didn't know. She, however, admired their strength in doing so.

Peering at her reflection again, she tucked several strands of her red hair, having escaped their pins, beneath Abram's hat. She then drank another swallow of water and took the flashlight and pail to the barn to milk the cow.

Inside the two-story structure, where the aroma of hay and manure permeated the crisp air, she sat on a stool beside the cow and rubbed her hands together to warm them. Few things angered Clara like having the cow kick the pail over from cold hands.

With her palms warm, she began milking. As the metallic rhythm of the twin streams struck the side of the pale, Clara grew drowsy. She once loved the misty feeling of sitting in the quiet of the barn and listening to Abram milking the cow. Although their Ordnung allowed many modern conveniences, they preferred growing their own food and having fresh milk for butter and cheese, which they sold from a stand near the mailbox when they had extra, along with vegetables from the garden. They had bought the house from an Amish family who belonged to a stricter Ordnung. Abram had planned to have the entire home wired when he hired a man to install the electric pump for the indoor plumbing. Instead, the money was needed to repair their old pickup truck, to repair the barn's roof, and to build a pig pen and a place for them to shelter when it rained and snowed. Unfortunately, Abram had fallen from the loft and broken his neck. Yes, they had spent the money on everything except the pigs, and Clara was glad. She didn't think she could kill and butcher one without Abram's help.

The cow mooed, jarring her from her thoughts. Outside, gravel crunched in the driveway. She knew only one person in this area, so it might be the neighbor arriving in his pickup truck. Standing, Clara girded herself for a confrontation.

Jonah Ellis was one of those men who refused to believe women were equal to men. Two weeks ago, when she, Edna, and John had stopped to rest on their walk from the local market about five miles away, Mr. Ellis had come along and stopped to insist he give them a ride home. Yes, his idea was practical, but the way he looked down at her from what was likely his six-foot plus height—she being a petite five-foot four inches and as slender as a newborn whitetail fawn—had angered her. It also hadn't helped the matter any that he wasn't Amish or Mennonite, or that his honey-brown eyes seemed to pluck her nerves, or that his wavy brown hair like Abram's had caught her eye, or that he lived with the woman he was engaged to. To Clara, living together out of wedlock was like the English saying: "Why buy the cow when you can get the milk for free?"

The vehicle door slammed. Footsteps crunched toward the house. Knuckles knocked on screened door. "Mrs. Engelman? It's Bishop Silverman."

Panic struck a harsh chord inside Clara's chest. Despite not caring what others thought of her wearing Abram's clothes, she didn't know what the bishop might say. More strands of her red hair hung from beneath Abram's hat. She tucked them in, made sure the zipper of his huge canvas coat was up, and left the barn.

As Abram's heavy boots clomped in the gravel, the bishop, about to knock on the door again, turned. "Clara?"

Not only did his look of disapproval slow Clara's stride, him calling her by her first name for the first time did as well. "I was milking the cow, Bishop Silverman." She wrapped her arms around herself. "It's very cold. That's why I'm wearing Abram's things."

A single twitch in the bishop's cheek showed his further disapproval. "I … well, I suppose you need to be warm."

Clara moved closer. Her breath, hard and fast, jetted from her nostrils in twin streams, the same as from the bishop's. "I would offer coffee," she said. "The children are still asleep and I hate to wake them."

"I understand. How are you— I mean, how are they doing?" His eyes darted to one side.

Unless Clara missed her guess, the bishop

was here for an unwelcome reason—one that her best friend, Alison Henley, had suggested he might attempt. Before Clara and Abram moved here, so Alison had said, the bishop's wife ran off with a man from town and filed for divorce a year later. Clara had never heard of a Mennonite man or woman divorcing. Regardless, she wasn't ready to marry again—if ever—and certainly not to Bishop Silverman.

The bishop cleared his throat. His face was red, either from the cold or embarrassment. He came closer. His hand raised to Clara's temple, where a single fingertip touched her skin. "I don't know how, but I never realized you have red hair." He licked his lips. "I came to ask—"

Clara backed away. "As you can see, I'm very busy."

"Do you need help with anything?"

"No, please. Why did you come?"

"I … well …"

Clara could see his intention in the way his eyes focused on hers. With Abram gone, the bishop had come to hover over her like a hawk seeking a mouse in the field of her mourning.

He raised his hand to her temple again. She wanted to run, to scream, to grab the pitchfork from the barn and make him leave. Instead, she simply stood there. If not, if he went back home and spread the word that he had caught her out of her dress and kapp, who knew what would happen.

The bishop withdrew his hand without touching her. "You have straw in your hair. I was only going to take it out."

Clara brushed at her hair; a piece of straw fell at her feet.

The bishop went to his pickup and returned with a huge pot covered with a lid. "This is cabbage soup I made last night. I enjoy cooking but I made too much, likely because I was thinking of my ... Well, Sarah's gone, but I can't stop thinking about her. I'm sure you feel the same way about Abram."

Shame heated Clara's cheeks. This poor

man missed his wife as much as she missed Abram, and he was only trying to help in any way he could. She took the pot. "Thank you for thinking of the children and me."

"You're welcome." He shoved his hands into his pants pockets. "You're right, it's very cold this morning."

Clara gave him the pot. "Please take that to the kitchen table while I get the milk I left in the barn. I'll make coffee to warm us up."

He took the pot. "I've been thinking about your situation here. You can't drive, and you live far away from our community." He paused. "You have a good neighbor in Jonah. I know him well and trust him. I'm sure he's willing to help around the farm if you need him."

Clara nodded. She could use help now and then, and it was kind of the bishop to make allowances for her situation, even for her English neighbor. Maybe she had misjudged Mr. Ellis when he had offered to give her and the children a ride. She went to the barn for the milk. In the kitchen, beside the table, the bishop faced her. "You said Edna and John are still asleep?"

Filling the percolator with water, Clara looked over her shoulder. "They still have nightmares about the funeral. Anytime they go near a hole outside, no matter how small, they run from it. I tried to explain death to them, and how they'll see their papa again, but they're too young to understand."

"Would you like me to try?" the bishop asked.

Clara noted the sincerity in his voice. "I'd rather not until they're older. They're starting to sleep better now." She finished filling the percolator, measured coffee, and took it to the stove.

Along with noting the bishop's sincere voice, she also noted the hint of gray hair at his temples, plus how he hadn't removed his wide-brimmed hat, black as a crow's breast feathers. She took Abram's coat and hat to the hanger, placed her kapp over her pinned hair, and returned to the stove, rubbing her cold hands together over the hot metal.

The bishop took her cue and hung his coat and hat on the peg beside hers, which caused a twinge of anger in her. It was as if he had taken Abram's place without asking, and she didn't like it at all. Despite her warming hands, she continued rubbing them together. Although the bishop seemed nice, she had the feeling he was watching her, possibly thinking of her as his future wife. Fear prickled along the back of her neck.

"Mrs. Engelman?"

Clara refused to turn. At least he had called her by her married name. "Yes?"

"If I'm making you uncomfortable by being here, I can leave."

His voice was soft and gentle. Shame heated Clara's cheeks again. Perhaps she was oversensitive because of losing Abram. She turned to face the patient man. "I admit it's strange having another man here with Abram gone." She paused to give her confused mind time to find the right words.

"I realize you're my bishop, but …" Her hands began to tremble. She raised them to her face and spun away to cry.

If her feelings about the bishop wanting her for a wife were true, she expected him to approach her, to touch her, perhaps to place a hand on her shoulder, but none of that happened.

Behind her, his footsteps shuffled on the hardwood floor. His clothing rustled as he donned his coat. More footsteps followed. The screened door softly closed, and the gravel crunched beneath the tires as he drove away.

Clara sank to her knees. Sobs continued to wrack her body until she had to force herself to stop or risk having a sore throat. Also, she needed to wake Edna and John soon, and she didn't want a raspy voice and reddened eyes to betray her tears.

She stood to the sound of percolating coffee. The aroma rose in the steam coming from the spout, reminding her of Abram again. He loved breakfast, particularly coffee. A pang of sorrow hit again, and Clara's sobs returned.

As much as she loved her sweet and gentle husband, how long would it take until she could treasure her memories of him with joy instead heartache?

The Essence of Emmaline Strong

The Blue Ridge Mountains of Virginia haven't always been a problem for me. In my Jeep 4x4 this morning, driving along its curvy roads, the sheer drop-offs to one side or the other tweaking my vertigo, I realized how I was only one turn away from oblivion.

Life's like that. There's no denying it, so why even try? It's not like I'm special enough to dodge oblivion.

Oblivion.

What a word.

The drive passed quickly—well, *too* quickly—and I arrived at the one place in the world I did *not* want to be. After all, who would want a follow-up appointment with a doctor of any kind, let alone an eye specialist after a zillion or so tests, plus one they took blood for and I forgot to ask why, being as nervous as a long-tailed cat in a room full of rocking chairs, a cow with a buck-toothed calf, or any one of a million other sayings like those we have in the south. At least my sense of humor hadn't totally left me, but it wasn't far from it.

In the waiting room, as I prayed over and over for my problem to not be what the specialist thought it was, a surreal feeling washes over me, as if my invisible words were bouncing off the ceiling and flying back at me, like my faith was a rubber ball and the ceiling was concrete. Considering everything I'd been through in the past two years—or in other words, chances at oblivion—I wouldn't be surprised. Still, I have a lot to be grateful for, but if this appointment went wrong, I might pull an epic wino drunk that would seriously upset my minister dad.

The vinyl chair squeaked when I crossed my blue jean-clad legs for the umpteenth time. I gave up and went to the single window overlooking the parking lot and imagined my town of Sufferer's Valley, tucked in mountains, and hoped it and my four-room house were firmly embedded in my mind's eye. That included my two five-string banjos, my acoustic guitar, and my last major purchase on plastic: a fine resonator guitar with flame-maple top, back, and sides, an ebony fretboard inlayed with mother of pearl diamonds, and a huge sound that blew me away the first time I played it.

Over two years ago, when I felt my life beginning to change in some horrible way, I either listened to or imagined the music and lyrics from some of my favorite musicians. Tony Rice would sing *Early Morning Rain*, *Song for a Winter's Night*, or play *Shenandoah* on his guitar, a 1935 Martin D-28, and my heart would slow from its runaway hammering deep inside my chest. More often than not, those wonderful melodies would do the trick. If not, Alison Krauss would sing *When You Say Nothing at all*, *Away Down the River*, or *Baby, Now That I've Found You*, and tears of joy would soothe me down to the marrow in my bones. For a newer member of the bluegrass movement, especially on the mandolin, I could always depend on Sierra Hull to send the blood roaring through my veins with the utter magic of her amazing touch on those eight strings, strung along such a small instrument, not to mention using her pure voice on tunes such as *Someone Like You, Summer's End*, and *Beautifully Out of Place.* Oh, and I can't forget Jerry Douglas playing *Hymn of Ordinary Motion* on one of his Beard resonator guitars, also known as a dobro. In my opinion, for the purest and sweetest tones that send me drifting away from life's troubles, it's hard to beat Jerry.

Yes, at this point in my life, I preferred slower, more poignant songs from those amazing artists. Given my situation, it made sense.

Shaking my head, I started to pray to be able to play my *own* instruments if the worst happened, but a door creaked open behind me. "Jordan, hon," the receptionist said, with her soft southern drawl, "you can come on back now." Another thing about the south: once you're on a first name basis with someone, mostly women, they add either "hon" or "sweetie" to the mix.

In the examination room, the doctor looked up from a notepad. "Hi, Jordan. Have a nice drive here this morning? The Blue Ridge certainly looks blue, doesn't it?"

I started to sit in the examination chair, but the doctor motioned me toward a normal chair next to the wall. I sat, and he rolled his chair closer. "Is your dad in the waiting room?"

Clamping my eyes shut, I swallowed. He would ask about Dad for one reason and one reason only. My heart jumped in my chest. I could hardly breathe. Before I realized I was crying, hot tears tracked down my cheeks.

"Jordan, is he here? Maybe your brother?"

I took a tissue from my purse and dabbed

my eyes. "Is it Best disease?"

"I'm afraid the genetic testing confirmed it."

So that was why they took my blood. How did I miss that when I'd spent an entire day on my PC researching my possible condition? So, I was going blind, and worse than that, no cure—not a single one—existed.

I looked up at the yellow tile ceiling, trying to pretend it wasn't there, trying to pretend blue skies filled the stuffy examination room, trying to pretend I was standing in the chilly pool beneath the waterfall up the mountain behind my house. Even if I were there, my prayers would bounce off those blue skies and slap me in the face.

Then again, my mom, God rest her soul, would have a thing or two to say about my situation:

Well, sweety, you just have to take it in stride and trust God. Besides, I'll be around to help you get through it.

No, Mom, I'd say. How can you be around when you died giving birth to Teddy? And you weren't there when I caught Tyler, that lying SOB, cheating on me in college either.

It's time to get over that, you know. Another fella will come 'round before you know it.

What guy would want a blind woman, Mom? I'll be stuck in my house at the base of Sufferer's Mountain. I won't be able to drive. I won't be able to teach my students to play banjo, guitar, or resonator guitar. I won't be able to get my groceries. I'll shrivel up and die, and the worst thing is how I won't have anyone to love. But hey, your life insurance came in handy when Dad helped me build that four-room shack I've got. See how much I've got to be grateful for? What's going blind compared to all that?

"Jordan, I know this is difficult."

I snapped out of my trance to face the doctor. "I think it's a little worse than difficult."

"You do have options, like special glasses. Gene therapy is promising, although it's a ways off yet. The best thing is to know what to expect. I'll tell you exactly that so it won't be too frightening."

The doctor went on to tell me how Best disease, also known as Best Vitelliform Dystrophy, was a type of juvenile macular degeneration. Then he said the one thing that completely made my day. "I'm not sure if you know this, but you should. It's inherited and can be passed on to children."

I bit my lower lip until the metallic taste of blood made me stop. I'd inherited this crap and shouldn't risk having children who might go blind like me. Just freakin' great, the final nail in the coffin, where my last threads of faith were laid to rest. First Mom, then Tyler, and now this, each a hammer banging those nails and me to my knees, where I'd never, ever, as long as I lived, pray again.

I stuffed the tissue in my purse and faced

the doctor. "I read on the internet that it's degenerative. How long do I have before I can't do anything for myself?"

"It's usually diagnosed in younger people," he said, crossing his arms. "Yours is already advanced. I'd say under five years, but it could be more or it could be less. Would you like to make an appointment to talk about your options?"

I hated to be rude, but I went straight to the receptionist, asked her to send me the bill, and sped with squealing tires around the mountain curves to Sufferer's Valley and its only grocery store—for six bottles of the cheapest wine I could afford.

At home, I drank one each for the next six nights. Following *that* bit of wisdom, between brief phone calls from Dad, when I told him what had happened and how I was fine, I did the same thing for six more nights, until I finally saw the light, so to speak, like the country song Hank Williams recorded back in 1948.

The light I saw? Waking up in pee-soaked jeans and a puke-soaked blouse that smelled of sour grapes was *not* fun.

Showered and dressed in clean jeans and a red-flannel shirt, I went to my music room and took my favorite picture of Mom from the table by the window, where the sun could highlight her blonde hair. When my brother, Josh, and I were kids, he teased me about how he'd inherited her hair and I'd inherited my mousy brown mess from Dad. Good thing I didn't get Dad's banjo-neck physique, thin as the proverbial rail, but I did inherit Mom's hourglass figure. Also like Mom, although I'm not crazy about it, I inherited her five-two height. Oh, well, it sucks to be me at times. Big duh.

Because of how I'd acted at the specialist's office, and my resulting sloppy drunkenness, Mom would kick my behind if she were here, and she'd have a durn good reason.

From the time I was about ten until I left home for college, I played banjo at a local gathering spot in town. I was twenty and had come home from college for the weekend when Dad took the picture. Mom and Josh were dancing, both grinning like maniacs, her blonde hair shining in the fluorescent lights. Her baby bump, which would've been Teddy, bulged like she carried quintuplets, and I was grinning too.

I put the picture back.

Did I get Best disease from Mom or Dad? Dad was safe because of his age, but Josh, being two years younger than me and likely wanting to marry and have kids one day, should be genetically tested.

On my PC, I entered a social networking site that Dad frequented for church news. The green icon said he was online, so I sent a message asking if he knew about Best disease being genetic. He responded that he did, adding how Josh was tested negative for the gene a few days after I told them about my diagnosis.

Dad began typing another message, and I

logged off the site. Lucky Josh, no worrying about passing on this nightmare to potential children. I clicked the PC to sleep, stood by the window, and there it was, the haze in my central vision.

My research said most patient's sight gradually deteriorated to 20-100, with 20-40 on the lower extreme and 20-200 on the upper end, what the medical community considered legally blind. The strangest part was how peripheral vision wasn't affected, but what good was that without central vision? Since the specialist had said the time to maximum sight loss was unknown, I'd head this crap off at the pass as much as I could, meaning I needed to make plans.

On the floor, I set my banjo case down, opened it, and ran my fingertips over the tailpiece, where the strings attach at the bottom, followed them all the way to the fifth string tuner for the shortest string, and kept going until I reached the four tuners on the peghead at the top of the neck. The feel of string and metal and wood was as familiar as my own body during a shower. Since I could shower with my eyes closed, I bet I could change strings on my banjo, dobro, and guitar with my eyes closed too.

With that problem conquered, what about teaching my students? I closed the banjo case, snapped the latches, and set it on its side. I could have them bring a digital recorder to record our lessons. Huh, about time something went my way.

I returned to the window. What about driving? Well, Dad would offer to chauffer my disabled self to the grocery store. The price I'd pay would be his caring suggestion to attend church, but that was better than starving to death.

Outside the window, beyond my backyard, the sloped beginning of Sufferer's Mountain rose over 2000 feet into the hazy clouds tinted with blue. Late October in the Blue Ridge. Oak, maple, and hickory trees on fire with red, orange, gold and every shade between. Unfortunately, my time to enjoy them was limited.

In my back jeans pocket, my phone played Dad's tone, the melody to *The Sweet Bye and Bye*. Oh sure, *now* my phone worked. The signal usually sucked because of the mountains, so why couldn't it suck now?

I swiped the screen. "What's up?"

"Hi, honey. I tried to catch you on the PC a minute ago but you logged off. What's the chance you can play banjo for my service at the nursing home in the morning? The folks would love to hear you."

Pinching the bridge of my nose, I considered his request. Sure, the folks there liked my playing, and I liked playing for them. "I'll be there at 9:30."

"Want to ride with me?"

"I can still drive."

"What about church? It's been a while since you've been, you know."

"My banjo needs new strings. I'll hear you at the nursing home anyway."

"It's not the same. You've got all night

to—"

"Breakfast in the morning."

"Doesn't take long."

"I'll sleep late."

"That's no better?"

I said nothing. I shouldn't have mentioned my sleep problems the last time we spoke.

"Maybe you should see a doctor about—"

"See you in the morning." I started to jab the end-call icon, but Dad said something I didn't catch. "What's that?"

"I said Josh will be in."

"I hope you two don't plan to gang up on me about my condition."

"He wants to. I told him to leave you alone."

"Tell him to pray about it." Durn, my faithless attitude in action. Besides, if my brother had driven all the way from the University of Virginia to visit, maybe I could get a few laughs out of him. He did that plenty when I broke up with the jerk in college, and finding humor where none existed pleased me to no end. Too bad I didn't have someone full-time to do that.

"You there, honey?"

"He could come with you to the nursing home."

"He's going out with friends tonight. Knowing him, he'll sleep in." Dad paused. "I thought I'd lost you."

Talk about double-meaning, as in the religious context of "being lost," which probably worried him concerning little old going-blind me. Still, I shouldn't have tried to end the call before he said goodbye. "I'll see him or I won't," I said. "Is he going back to school after church?"

"He mentioned it."

"That's the best I can do."

"How about coming for lunch around one? I haven't seen you in two weeks."

I waited for the rest. *And you only live on the other side of town*. I wanted to ask why he hadn't stopped by, but he'd likely been visiting "the sick and the shut-ins," practicing with the choir, holding Wednesday night Bible study and writing sermons. I told him I had some banjo lessons to plan for Monday and stuck the phone back in my jeans.

In the kitchen, I poured white wine for a change and raised the glass. "Here's to you, Josh. I'm sincerely happy you can continue our lineage without being afraid your children will go blind."

I sipped. "Maybe your future wife will have a brother who doesn't mind having a blind wife." I downed the semi-sweet liquid in one huge gulp. "Who doesn't mind if she shouldn't have kids either."

After an early dinner of a ham sandwich and tomato soup from a can, including another glass of wine, I channel-surfed until rain pattered against the living room window. In the music room again, I went to the window. The reddening leaves on the maple in the backyard trembled with a slight breeze. Midway up the mountain, barely illuminated by the dimming twilight, the breeze bent the fog to its will.

Like blindness was bending my life to *its* will.

Maybe tomorrow would start clear, with a gorgeous sunrise over the peaks to the east. I needed light to lift me, a beautiful red dawn to send my sadness scampering away like a kitten I once had.

I went back to the living room, plopped to the sofa, and thumbed the remote.

Huh. Not with *my* luck.

About the Author

J. Willis Sanders lives in southern Virginia, with his wife and several stringed instruments.

With twelve novels published and more on the way, he enjoys crafting intriguing characters with equally intriguing conflicts to overcome. He also loves the natural world, and, more often than not, his stories include those settings. Most also utilize intense love relationships and layered themes.

His first idea for a novel is a ghostly World War II era historical that takes place mostly in the midwestern United States, which utilizes some little-known facts about German POW camps there at the time. It's the first of a three-book series, in which characters from the first book continue their lives.

Although he loves history, he has written several contemporary novels as well, and some include interesting paranormal twists, both with and without religious themes.

He also loves the Outer Banks of North Carolina, and he has written three novels within different time frames based on the area, what he calls his Outer Banks of North Carolina Series. (Yes, they've been published, and he has more story ideas about the area.)

Also, he enjoys learning about the variations of Amish culture, which inspired his Eliza Gray and Clara Engelman series.

Other hobbies include reading (of course), vegetable gardening, playing music with friends, and songwriting, some of which are in a few of his novels.

To follow his work, visit any of these websites:

https://jwillissanders.wixsite.com/writer

https://www.facebook.com/J-Willis-Sanders-874367072622901

https://www.amazon.com/J-Willis-Sanders/e/B092RZG6MC?ref_=dbs_p_ebk_r00_abau_000000

Readers: to help those considering a purchase, please leave a review on Amazon.com, Goodreads.com, or wherever you bought this book.
They help authors more than you may realize.

Thank you.

Printed in Great Britain
by Amazon

15705313R00133